GUN TRAIL

Center Point
Large Print

GUN TRAIL

Mack Saunders

CENTER POINT LARGE PRINT
THORNDIKE, MAINE

This Center Point Large Print edition
is published in the year 2025 by arrangement with
Golden West Inc.

Copyright © 1956 by Graphic Publishing Company, Inc.

All rights reserved.

The text of this Large Print edition is unabridged.
In other aspects, this book may vary
from the original edition.
Printed in the United States of America
on permanent paper sourced using
environmentally responsible foresting methods.
Set in 16-point Times New Roman type.

ISBN: 979-8-89164-519-6

The Library of Congress has cataloged this record
under Library of Congress Control Number: 2024951729

1

Rock Wesley took delivery of the horses in the railroad yard at Winslow. He had brought Stu Henley and Vic Anderson with him to help in the drive to his ranch near Silver Springs. Stu had been skeptical about this latest venture of his, but after one glimpse of the Morgans, he was sold. His eyes brightened and he gave a low, appreciative whistle. "Man, what horseflesh! They're worth every cent they cost you, Rock."

"That's the way I figured it," Rock answered. "If we're going to raise horses, we might as well do it right. A couple years from now, we'll really be in business."

He had a horse ranch up on the high mesas and a dozen men trapping and breaking wild mustangs. He had a good market for such horses right here in the territory, at various cattle ranches, but an even better market existed. The Army always needed horses. Army specifications, however, were hard to meet. He thought this would do it—the Morgan strain added to the mustang should produce the wiry but manageable horse the Army wanted.

They left Winslow that afternoon, angling

across country to the north and west. Rock had been afraid of some trouble on the way, that after their long confinement in cattle cars the Morgans might be restive and want to run, but they didn't. And when the men made their camp that night, Rock was more pleased than he wanted to admit. It had taken every cent he could raise to buy these brood mares, but the risk was going to be worth it.

After the horses had been staked out for the night, he and Stu and Vic sat around their fire and talked. Rock had known Stu Henley from boyhood, and Vic Anderson longer than that. Vic had worked for the elder Wesley and had not been enthusiastic about Rock's changing the place over to a horse ranch—he was a man who never liked change. His disagreement with Rock had not, however, made any difference in his loyalties.

"We'll head due north tomorrow," Rock suggested, "then swing west the next day, skirt the Modoc Valley and cut through the Temple Hills. That way we'll miss most of the rough country. It may take a little longer, but there's no rush."

"I'll bet those Morgans could take any kind of country, any kind of rush," Stu said.

Stu had fallen in love with them.

"I had a horse, once, that was a quarter Morgan," Vic said. "Good horse, too. I could run him all day and when it came to cutting a herd he couldn't be topped."

They went on talking, mostly about horses, finally drew straws to settle who was to take the first, second, and third watch during the night. Rock wasn't convinced any kind of guard was necessary, but the Morgans were too valuable for him to take a chance.

He drew the first watch himself and, after the others had turned in, lit his pipe and made a brief inspection of the herd, then came back to the fire. He was tall, with wide, sloping shoulders and a wiry body. He had dark eyes, dark hair, and a face that was too narrow, too thin and bony. Chasing wild horses and breaking them to the saddle didn't help a man put on weight. He could have carried thirty more pounds comfortably, but he felt good, ate well, and had almost perfect muscular coordination.

The purchase of the Morgan brood mares was the fourth important step in his career. The first had come when he was eighteen, and when his father had said to him, "Rock, you're a grown man and supposed to be responsible for what you do. If you've got yourself into trouble with Nels Bergstrom, it's up to you to work it out the best way you can. Don't come running to me." In a bloody fight he never would forget, he had settled his quarrel with the neighbor's son. The second step in his career had come with his father's death, five years ago, when he had decided to hold the ranch rather than sell it. The third important milestone had been passed two years ago, when he had sold his cattle and started raising horses. There nearly had been one more. Three years ago he had been desperately in love with a girl in Sawtelle. He had wanted to marry her and take her to his ranch, but things hadn't worked out that way. He was getting over it, now. The memory didn't hurt him as much as it once had.

Rock added more wood to the fire, then sat down near it. He glanced at the silent figures of Stu Henley and Vic Anderson. He had two good men in Stu and Vic, and a third one, just as loyal, back at the ranch. Jeff Elliott. He had two crews out in the hills who had working arrangements with him and in an emergency might be counted on, but Stu, Vic and Jeff were the three he depended on, and he was lucky in the kind of men they were. He had stretched himself more than he should have in buying these Morgans, but he had a crew to stand by him if things were hard for a time.

They rode on again shortly after dawn, heading due north this time, and avoiding the rugged, hilly country to the west, and the day passed without incident. It was on the next day, and when they were riding west, skirting the Modoc

Valley, that they met the two men—tall, gaunt, bearded fellows who said they worked for Arne Chenoweth.

"Nice horses you got there," one of them mentioned. "Where you taking them?"

"Up to our ranch, on Rolling Mesa," Rock answered.

"Where's that?"

"Near Sawtelle, three days' ride from here."

The man nodded. "They wouldn't be for sale, would they? Arne's in the market for horses."

"These aren't for sale," Rock told him. "I have other horses for sale."

"Then why don't you drop by an' see Arne? His place ain't far out of your way. Dip south a little as you're headin' west and you'll run right into it."

"I may do that," Rock said vaguely.

He didn't like the way the two men kept looking at the Morgans. He felt sharply on guard. And after the unkempt pair rode on he watched them out of sight, aware of a growing uneasiness.

"Two nice characters," Stu said under his breath. "If they'd been six instead of two, we might have lost our horses."

"We still might," Rock said. "We didn't skirt the Modoc Valley wide enough."

"Then you've heard of this Arne Chenoweth?"

"Yes, I've heard of him. There are a dozen

ranches in the Modoc Valley, but only one that counts. Arne Chenoweth is the Modoc, both valley and town. I've been told he makes his own laws, rules the place like a king. He heads a tough crew and does as he pleases. The Modoc Valley is a good place to stay away from."

"We can angle more to the north," Vic suggested.

"We're going to," Rock said. "And we're going to move faster."

They did, and saw no other men that day. By the time they made their night camp, some of Rock's uneasiness had worn off. Chenoweth, he reasoned, might be a law unto himself in the Modoc where people had come to accept it. But that shouldn't necessarily mean that he would risk anything crude on the outside.

"We could stand a double guard tonight," Stu offered. "Or for that matter, we could keep traveling. We've got a moon."

Rock shook his head. "Just keep your rifle handy, Stu. But I doubt you'll need it."

The night was quiet and again they got an early morning start. Toward noon they were driving up a long, narrow fold in the hills when the firing started.

It came from the trees to their left. At the head of the string of horses, Vic stiffened in his saddle, then pitched to the ground. Rock reined up. He felt the crease of a bullet burn across his chest.

Another lifted his hat from his head. He shouted an unnecessary warning to Stu Henley as he reached for his rifle and drew it from its boot. Out of the corner of his eye he saw Stu weaving from side to side in the saddle, like a man who had had too much to drink.

He stared at the trees from where the shots were coming, and saw only trees—there was nothing to fire at. A blow ripped against the side of his head so sharply it blinded him. He felt his horse leap forward, and held on for a while, but the stabbing, blinding pain in his head smothered his senses. He didn't know when he fell. For a long time, he didn't know anything.

His awareness returned slowly. It was growing dark. Rock tried to sit up but a sudden wave of dizziness nullified the effort. After a time he found the gash in his scalp. It was above his ear and temple; it was deep and still bleeding a little. The side of his face was matted with dried blood. He untied his neckerchief, then wound it around his head and under his chin. He tore off a piece of his shirt, rolled it up, and fitted it in the gash, under the neckerchief. The makeshift bandage hurt and was unsanitary, but it might help stop the bleeding.

By now, it was fully dark. He waited for the moon to come up, and while he waited he thought back over what had happened. He and

Stu and Vic had accepted delivery of fifteen Morgan mares in Winslow. A dozen men, there, had seen and admired the horses, but no one had followed them when they left Winslow, and on their way north and west they had run into no one but Chenoweth's two riders. From those bare facts and from what he knew of Chenoweth, it was easy to reach a conclusion. This was on the border of Chenoweth's range where his word was law. The deadly ambush they had run into had been neatly set up by men who knew this country and had been planned not only to take the Morgans but to eliminate all trace of the men driving them. The merciless firing from the trees was proof of that. They hadn't been given a chance to surrender their horses. Stu and Vic, he was sure, were dead. That he had escaped was pure chance—something to think about later. Perhaps he hadn't escaped.

He struggled to his feet after the moon came up. He didn't know the country, or why he was alive. There might be a ranch over the next hill, or the closest ranch might be Chenoweth's, but he would have to take a chance on that. He couldn't stay here. He had to get to a place where he could have his head properly bandaged and where he could borrow a horse, and food. His best bet lay in heading toward Modoc and hoping he could find one of the small ranches in this end of the valley.

His first steps were uncertain and he fell several times, but each time got to his feet again, and moved on. After a while he grew steadier, and for what seemed like hours he walked in what he thought was a fairly straight line to the south. He came to a stream where he drank, bathed his face and hands, and rested. Then he walked on, climbing the low ridge ahead and dropping into the valley below.

Somewhere toward morning, his mind started wandering and his feet grew heavy and started tripping, and finally, when he fell, he couldn't get up.

The sun, beating down on his shoulders, awoke him. He got up and stumbled on, not sure now where he was going, or why. He fell, got up, and fell again. A bird wheeled in the sky, high overhead. It was joined by another, then a third. They circled lower and lower until Rock, lying motionless, could hear the beat of their wings. He turned on his side and saw them and cursed them in words that came from a sand-dry throat and were scarcely louder than a whisper. He got up and staggered on until he fell again. This time, when he heard the sound of the birds, he had no strength to swear at them.

He tried desperately to cling to a fringe of consciousness but the hammering pain in his head seemed to be growing worse. He closed his eyes, promising himself he would close them for only a moment or two.

One of the buzzards lighted on a nearby rock and sat there, watching him silently. Another dropped down, closer. The third made a circling dive just above his head.

2

Meg McAlpin had spent the night with her married sister in Modoc. In the morning they continued the argument they had dropped the night before. Alice was married to Charlie Weston, and was quite satisfied with her status as a wife. She seemed determined that Meg should take a similar step.

"I think you're out of your mind to say no to a man like Jim Fleming," she declared. "He's young, and he has his own ranch, and he's as steady as they come."

"But I don't want to get married," Meg said.

"What about Arne Chenoweth? If you used your influence on him—"

"Never."

"You've got to marry someone, Meg."

"Why?"

"What else is there for a woman?"

Meg laughed. "I can go on working the ranch with father. I enjoy it, really. What do I want with a man?"

Alice looked at her frowning. "Don't you ever want a man? Wouldn't you like to have a baby?"

"If I want a baby I know how to get one," Meg said lightly. She laughed again at the almost startled look that came into her sister's face.

"Don't worry about me, Alice. I'm getting along all right. Really I am."

The argument continued while they did the breakfast dishes and then while Alice bathed the baby. Alice was twenty-four and was carrying her second child, but still looked almost as girlish as the day she was married. Meg, two years younger, had the same, slender figure, but a thinner face. She never would be as pretty as Alice, she thought, but the thought did not bother her.

After the baby's bath, Meg went out to the barn to saddle up for her return ride to the ranch. Alice joined her in the yard when she was ready to leave.

"I didn't mean it about Arne Chenoweth," she said earnestly. "I wouldn't want you to marry Arne—but give Jim another chance."

"He never had the first one," Meg said. "Quit pushing me, Alice. I'm perfectly happy as things are."

She climbed into the saddle, waved to her sister, and rode around the side of the house to the street. She was wearing a black, divided riding skirt, a tan blouse, and had her hair tucked up under a broad-brimmed man's hat. Her skin was nicely tanned.

Arne Chenoweth waved to her from the porch of Wahlberg's store as she rode up Main Street and she stopped her horse. He stepped off the porch and strode toward her. He was a big, thick-bodied man, close to his prime. He had ruddy cheeks, sharp, dark eyes, and his hair was beginning to show iron gray. When he wanted to, he could be quite pleasant, and he seemed in the mood this morning.

"You're not leaving town just when I get here, are you?" he asked, smiling. "I wish you could stay for a while—have dinner with me."

Meg shook her head. "Sorry, Arne, but father expects me home by noon."

"Disappoint him, just this once."

"I'm afraid I've disappointed him many times," Meg said.

She was conscious of the three men watching her from the porch of the store, as well as others on down the street. The three on the porch were Ollie Reed, Jake Laydon, and Abe Roebuck, and between them, they made the hard core of Chenoweth's crew. They were rough, violent men. Some people in the valley and a few in town said that Arne Chenoweth, himself, wasn't so bad, and that much that was attributed to him could be more properly blamed on the men who rode for him. How much truth was in that, Meg didn't know, but there certainly were times when Arne could seem gracious and friendly and wholly unlike the men who rode for him.

"I wish you'd change your mind," he said, still smiling. "But I know you too well to think you will. Are you coming to the dance, Saturday night?"

Meg said, "Father may want to come in Saturday. If he does, I might come with him."

She rode on, still conscious of the men on the store porch and of the others on the street who had witnessed her encounter with Arne Chenoweth, and aware that everyone knew of Arne's interest in her, and that some would try to guess at what they had talked about. For some reason, she felt a little annoyed at herself.

She passed Roy Seigel's office. Roy was standing in front of it. He was a tall, thin, bold young man, and one of the few in Modoc who was almost openly defiant of Arne Chenoweth. She waved to him and, after a momentary hesitation, Roy waved back.

Beyond the town, Meg let her horse run until he was winded, then crossed the Modoc River at a slower pace and angled through the hills toward her father's ranch. She felt strangely uneasy and, after studying her thoughts for a time, decided that the reason for her troubled mind lay in the argument she had had with Alice and the way she had resisted her sister's suggestion that she get married. The father of her children . . .

This brought Jim Fleming to her mind. He was young and steady, just as Alice had said, and she rather liked him. But she didn't want to marry Jim—or anyone—for a long time. A man she scarcely had known had spoiled her for marriage. A man who had come here three years before, and who had stayed in Modoc only three days—a man named Art Kellner.

She was sometimes amazed at the vividness with which she could recall Art Kellner, and at the way he had affected her life. Long ago, trying to analyze it, she had decided that she hadn't fallen in love with Art, but that she would have fallen in love with him if he had lived, and had stayed in Modoc Valley. What had happened to spoil that had happened with the suddenness that was characteristic of the time and place. Art Kellner, three days after his arrival in Modoc, had run into an argument with a man named Dutch Wyman, one of Chenoweth's riders. There had been a gunfight, and Art Kellner's life had run out in the dust of the street.

Dutch Wyman still rode for Chenoweth. Every time Meg saw him she felt a violent emotional reaction. Once she even had thought of marrying Arne just so she could influence him to the point of firing Dutch Wyman and chasing him out of the valley, but she quickly got over that. No, she wasn't marrying anyone—at least for a long time.

She rode on, and half an hour from her father's ranch saw the buzzards circling high in the sky and a little off to the left. She instinctively swung her horse in that direction. The buzzards had dropped quite low by the time she was near, and were settling down while she still was half a mile away. She lifted her horse to a gallop. She had no idea what it was the buzzards were stalking. Not until they flew away, when she was quite close, did she recognize the motionless figure on the ground as that of a man.

Reining up, she swung down and hurried to his side. She was sure he was dead. When she rolled him over and saw the blood and dirt on his face, she was positive of it, and huddled above him, breathless, shocked, bewildered, and a little frightened. She stared at him, wondering who he was and how he had come here. It was hard to tell what he really looked like. The blood and dirt and whiskers on his face, and the pallor underlying the tan of his skin made him seem old, but his hair was as dark as hers.

His eyes rolled open. He didn't look at her, didn't look anywhere. Meg stood up, shuddering. She had heard somewhere that a man's eyes opened after he died. She glanced down the valley and saw with a quick feeling of relief that her father was riding this way. He, too, must have seen the circling birds. She looked at the man again and caught her breath. He was staring up at her—his lips were moving.

She knelt down beside him.

"Thanks for chasing those birds away," he whispered. "I'll—get up again in a minute."

"You'll do nothing of the sort," Meg said.

"You've been badly wounded. You'll lie right where you are until father gets here."

She felt suddenly quite weak and shaky, which she knew was ridiculous.

Rock Wesley was only vaguely conscious of being helped to mount a horse, and of being held in the saddle for the ride to the McAlpin ranch. He didn't remember being undressed and put to bed, and was completely unaware of the slow and careful job Ed McAlpin did on the wound in his scalp and another raw gash across his chest. When he woke up again and the girl seated near his bed told him he had been sleeping for a day and a half, he wouldn't believe it.

"What time is it?" he demanded.

"Eight in the morning."

"I want to borrow a horse," Rock said. "And some food, if you can let me have some food."

"Aren't you sort of rushing things?" the girl asked. "Father thinks you ought to take it easy for a couple of days."

He shook his head. "I've already wasted too much time. If you'll get my clothes—"

The girl didn't answer him. She smiled and picked up the sewing in her lap.

"Did you hear me?" Rock asked irritably.

"I heard you," the girl said. She did not move from her chair.

Rock glared at her. He guessed her age at about

twenty. She was a mite thin but didn't have an unpleasant face and there was a tantalizing twinkle in her eyes.

Rock sat up, and immediately regretted it. His head started hammering; he had to close his eyes against a sudden dizziness.

"You'll feel much better tomorrow, Mr. Wesley," the girl said.

He gave her another angry look. "How do you happen to know my name?"

"It was on some letters which fell out of your pocket when we carried you in. To make things even, I'm Meg McAlpin. My father's name is Ed McAlpin. And you at present are at the McAlpin ranch which is north and east of Modoc."

Rock lay down again in the bed. He managed a smile and said, "I remember you now, Meg. You chased the buzzards away."

"Father got there at almost the same time," Meg said. "He saw them, too. I was on my way back from town."

"How far from here did you find me?"

"About three miles up the valley."

"I wonder how far I walked."

"From where?"

"From where—I was shot."

His eyes darkened and he could feel his muscles growing tense. He thought of Stu Henley and Vic Anderson—the buzzards would have had an easy time with them, but it was more likely that the raiders had buried them. His mind was not yet functioning clearly, but he remembered hanging on to his horse—his horse must have carried him away.

"Do you want to tell me about it?" Meg asked.

Rock made a restless motion with his arm. "There's so little to tell."

"No matter how little—you can't blame my father and me for being curious. We don't need people wounded by bullets. When we first saw you and realized you were a stranger, we thought you might be one of the outlaws from back in the Temple Hills. Then the letters fell out of your pocket and we saw the address. Sawtelle. Father says that's a small town up in the mesa country, far north and west of here."

"I've a horse ranch near there."

"How did you get so far from home?"

"I—and two of my men—took delivery on some Morgan brood mares in Winslow. We were driving them toward the mesa country when—we lost them."

The girl had stopped sewing. She was leaning forward, her body tense. He grinned a little, bleakly.

"We ran into an ambush," he said. "We didn't even catch a glimpse of the men who were shooting at us. They were hidden by the trees. The two men with me were killed, I think. The horse I was riding ran away and I managed to

23

hang on. He must have dropped me—far enough away for the drygulchers not to find me. Or I wouldn't be here today."

Meg's eyes had widened. Her breath was coming fast. She laid aside her sewing, stood up, left the room and came back a moment later with a steaming cup of coffee. She held it out to Rock, saying, "Here, I think you need this."

"I need more than coffee," Rock said. "I need a horse and rifle."

Meg straightened. "So you can find the men who stole the brood mares? So you can let them finish what they started?" Now she sounded angry.

"What would you have me do?" Rock asked. "The two men who were killed weren't just two hired hands. They were like brothers to me." He was embarrassingly aware of speaking of intimate matters, something this girl couldn't possibly understand. "Should I forget how they died?"

"Not looking for a fight is one way to live longer," Meg said, her voice so low he hardly caught the words.

"But who wants to live like that?"

"You'd be surprised how many people do."

"Not me," Rock said.

She turned her eyes from his, looking troubled and uncertain.

"At least you don't have to go rushing off like a

madman," she said finally. "You could do a little planning, first."

Rock's eyes narrowed thoughtfully. "What planning?"

"I don't know. I just think it's good to have a plan, no matter what you're up against."

"I've got a plan," Rock said. "I mean to find the men who ambushed us, and bring them to justice."

Meg shook her head. "That's not a plan. It's a purpose. A plan would involve a way to go about it."

Rock turned on his side to stare at her. He could sense the good, solid reasoning behind what she was saying, and made an attempt to bring the problem he was facing into a clearer focus.

"What you are telling me, is this," he suggested. "I should measure what I am up against, then figure out what I can do about it."

"Something on that order."

"That means, you know something about it. Want to tell me what you're thinking?"

She shook her head. "I don't know anything. Your first step should be to report what has happened to the sheriff, in Modoc."

"Is the sheriff Chenoweth's man?"

Meg frowned. "What do you know about Arne Chenoweth?"

"Only what I've heard—that he's the big man in this Modoc. That his word is law."

"It isn't that bad," Meg said uneasily. "There are people who swear his word is good. There are others who oppose him."

"Two of his riders met us the day before the ambush. We saw no one else since leaving Winslow."

"And because of that you would blame the ambush on Arne Chenoweth."

"Because of that, I'd be suspicious of him."

Meg bit her lip. She looked at him, then looked quickly away. "Be suspicious all you want to," she said slowly. "But think carefully before you accuse a man of murder and horse stealing. And if it's Arne Chenoweth you mean to accuse—don't unless you have proof—"

She broke off and raised her head at the sound of someone riding into the yard, then got to her feet and walked to the window. "It's father," she said, and hurried from the room.

Rock reached for the coffee which he had set on the stand near his bed. It was cool enough to drink and tasted good. He finished it, put back the cup, then stretched out and reviewed his talk with the girl.

Her advice had been sensible. He had to admit that, yet he couldn't escape the feeling that she had been holding something back in her talk with him—that she hadn't been completely honest. He was scowling at the ceiling when Ed McAlpin came into the room.

McAlpin had a tall, rangy figure, and was quite thin. His hair was gray and his eyes, as dark as Meg's, were buried in deep wells in his head. He nodded his greeting and asked, "Feeling better, Wesley?"

"Much better," Rock said.

"Meg tells me you and two others were driving some brood mares across country near here when you ran into a rustlers' ambush."

"That's what happened."

"I suppose you want to get to Modoc soon as you can to report it to the sheriff."

"I'd like to go back to where we ran into the ambush first. I want to take a look at the place."

"We'll ride there tomorrow."

"Why not this afternoon? It can't be far from here."

"Think you'll be up to it?" When he saw the look on Rock's face, McAlpin shrugged. "All right. This afternoon. We'll head for Modoc in the morning. Any idea who the outlaws were?"

"No proof of who they were, if that's what you mean."

"Proof's a damned important thing, Wesley."

"Then I'll get it."

McAlpin was staring at him soberly. After a moment he nodded. "I hope you do, Wesley. I sure hope you do."

He sounded as though he meant it.

3

They rode up the meadow that afternoon to the place where Meg had found him, and from there followed his trail north. It was less than five miles to the valley where the ambush had occurred, and this surprised Rock. He had been sure he had walked several times that far.

The trail of the stolen mares led due west from the point of ambush, and at a guess, six or eight riders had been with them. The trail, now, was three days old, but was well enough marked to be followed, and the temptation to strike out and see where it led was almost too hard to resist.

"It's a clear trail right now," McAlpin said. "But farther on it'll be blotted. You can be positive of that. The men who took your mares have had two days to cover up what happened to them. Even if they figured you were dead, I'll bet they didn't take any chances."

"Blotted?" Rock asked. "How will it be blotted?"

"Chenoweth's range reaches up almost this far. He has several large herds of cattle in the hills west of here. A few men could start some of those cattle over the trail left by your mares, and hide it forever. It's an old trick we've run into before in this part of the country."

"You mean there's been other rustling?"

"Some outlaws are supposed to have a hide-out north of here."

"I never heard of any outlaws in the Temple Hills," Rock said.

"You don't live here," McAlpin answered. "Where did the shooting start?"

"From those trees, over that way."

They rode toward the trees where the outlaws had been hidden before the ambush and found where horses had recently been tethered, and unmistakable signs of several men waiting. The earth was trampled and cigarette butts littered the ground.

They found one other thing—a mound of fresh earth covered by leaves and dead branches—a mound marking what Rock was sure was a double grave. He didn't open it. He would leave that job for the sheriff's posse.

Meg said very little while they were in the valley or on their way back home, and she was silent that evening, at supper. McAlpin, too, seemed lost in his own thoughts. It was clear to Rock that what had happened so close to their ranch had had a sobering effect on them. When they looked at him they seemed distinctly uneasy.

"I've got to figure one of two things," he said abruptly. "Some outlaw band may have ambushed us. If that's what happened, they may drive the mares out of this part of the country, fast as they can. Or it may have been some crowd here in the valley that ambushed us. In that case, they may be holding the mares where they think I won't find them. Which possibility do you think most likely, McAlpin?"

McAlpin cleared his throat. "Hard to guess about a thing like this, but no man likes to think a neighbor would be guilty of something like you ran into."

"What if you were in my shoes?"

"I'm glad I'm not, Wesley."

"But if you were?"

"I'd go to the sheriff, as we planned. That's your first step, no matter what the truth of the matter may be."

Meg stared at her plate. "It was the outlaws in the Temple Hills who planned the ambush," she said under her breath. "It couldn't have been anyone living in the valley."

Her words were quite direct but from her tone of voice she seemed to be trying to convince herself of the truth of her statement.

Shortly after dawn, they set out for Modoc. Rock still had occasional twinges of pain from his wounds, but he felt much steadier than yesterday.

Mostly they rode in silence—McAlpin and his daughter showed the same reluctance to talk this morning, as the night before. Inner worries seemed to be troubling them. An inescapable conclusion came to Rock Wesley—McAlpin and his daughter knew, or thought they knew, who was responsible for the ambush, and this guilty knowledge was smothering them like a heavy blanket.

When they came within sight of the town, Meg looked over at him and said, "Don't do anything rash, Mr. Wesley. Don't push things. You're a stranger in Modoc and the people here have never been very friendly to strangers."

"In other words, walk softly." Rock grinned.

Meg nodded. "We used to have an old man working for us who had a saying. It went something like this. 'Life may be hard, but it's worth hanging on to. When you die, you die for a long time.' I'd think about that if I were you."

That she was warning him against something she didn't feel free to discuss couldn't have been any clearer.

Modoc was a cluster of buildings around two rows of stores and business houses facing each other across a narrow, dusty street. Some of the stores had false fronts, a few had wood slat awnings over the boardwalk, a few boasted porches. Rock counted three saloons, a hotel, feed store, a restaurant, barber shop, bank and grocery store before they came to the sheriff's office and pulled up at the tie-rail in front of it. He noticed only a few other saddled horses on the street and saw only two men dressed as cowhands. It was too early in the day for many men to have come in from the range.

A fat man with hulking shoulders appeared in the doorway to the sheriff's office as they dismounted. He had puffy cheeks and several chins too many. There was a friendly, almost jovial expression on his face. He called out, "Meg, you're beautiful as ever. Why don't you come in to see me more often?" And then he added, "Howdy, Ed," and looked curiously at Rock.

"Henry, this is Rock Wesley, a horse rancher from the high mesa country near Sawtelle," McAlpin said. "Wesley, this is Henry Sale, our sheriff."

Rock acknowledged the introduction, shaking the sheriff's plump hand, then dropping it and following him into the office. Meg and her father joined them.

"Wesley, here, has a story to tell you," McAlpin said.

The sheriff grinned at Rock. "Then, let's have it. Just remember I'm an old man and don't like to ride any more than I have to."

Rock wasn't quite sure of what he thought of the sheriff. As briefly as possible, he explained what had happened in the meadow above the McAlpin ranch.

Sale didn't get excited or look surprised, but a scowl shadowed his face. Finally he looked at McAlpin and said, "That outlaw band from the

Temple Hills, Ed. Some day they'll reach too far down into the valley, and we'll get them?"

"Some day?" Rock asked.

The sheriff nodded. "That's what I said, Wesley. Oh, I'll get a posse together, and we'll take a ride up there, but the trail will peter out before we catch up with the outlaws. They've had several days to hide it, and they're good at trail blotting. This has happened to me before."

"What if it wasn't the outlaws from the Temple Hills?" Rock asked.

Sale stiffened. "I don't get it, Wesley. What are you driving at? We may have a few men in the valley who wouldn't hesitate to pick up a few extra horses if they could, but I don't know anyone who would go as far as murder to accomplish it."

"Those horses weren't ordinary horses," Rock said. "They were blooded Morgans. Mares I meant to use for breeding."

"I still don't know anyone in the Modoc who would shoot men down to get them. Want to ride with my posse tomorrow?"

"Tomorrow? Why wait until tomorrow?"

"Couldn't get much of a posse together right now," the sheriff said. "Ain't many range men in town. Besides, this trip may involve several days of riding, and the fellows who will go with us have got to make plans to get away."

"I'll be one," McAlpin said.

"Fine." The sheriff nodded.

Rock tried to mask his disappointment. He knew that another day might not make much difference on a trail that already was cold, but the sheriff's casual way of going about this was hard to take. Nor did he like the assumption that the outlaws were known, and that they were some vague band hiding out in the hills.

McAlpin had stood up and turned to the door. "I'll see you again before I leave town, Sale," he promised.

"Fine. See you in the morning, about dawn," the sheriff said, glancing at Rock. "Or maybe I'll see you around town."

"I'll be around," Rock said.

He followed Meg and her father outside. McAlpin must have sensed the frustrated anger building up in him, for he said soothingly, "Maybe Sale could have moved a little faster, but after all, you'll be following a cold trail."

"It'll be colder by tomorrow," Rock said.

"Maybe," McAlpin conceded. "Maybe." He seemed to want to add something more, but didn't.

"Do you want to stay with us tonight?" Meg asked. "You and father could join the posse in the morning."

"No, I'll stay here in town," Rock said. "Can I use the horse I rode in on?"

"Glad to let you use him," McAlpin said.

Rock put out his hand. He said, "Mr. McAlpin, when this is all over, I hope to be able to thank you and your daughter more properly for what you did for me."

"Forget it," McAlpin said. "You coming with me, Meg?"

"No, I'll see you later," Meg said.

He scowled at her, and seemed suddenly uneasy, but after a brief hesitation, he moved off down the street.

Rock looked at Meg, and saw her frown again. "You're disappointed, aren't you?" she said. "You wanted the sheriff to get a posse and chase into the hills right away."

"That's part of it," Rock admitted. "But another thing I don't like is his assurance that he knows who he's after."

"You think—"

"I'm not sure the outlaws from the Temple Hills are guilty—if there are any outlaws up there."

"You mean you're still jumping at conclusions."

"I'm not jumping at anything. The sheriff jumped at a conclusion. You saw him."

Meg bit her lip. "If you're going to stay here in town, I want to tell you something."

"Go ahead."

"It's about—Arne Chenoweth."

"Good."

"The sheriff used to work for him, and there are others here in town who used to be on

Chenoweth's Arrowhead ranch. The man at the livery stable, the fellow who runs the blacksmith shop, and Dick Sommers at the feed store. But that's only part of it. Arne Chenoweth owns those three places. He owns three of the four saloons in Modoc, and he owns the hotel. I don't mean that all the people here love him. Some don't. Some hate him. But word of what happens and what is said always gets back to him."

"You're telling me not to talk out of turn?"

The girl took a deep breath. "I'll be more blunt than that. If you knew it was Chenoweth who was responsible for stealing your horses, and if you had the proof, there's only one safe thing you could do—run. And I mean it, Mr. Wesley. If you have a family—"

"I don't have a family."

"You still would be wise to run."

He glanced along the street. Several riders had turned into town from one of the north roads and were heading down the street toward them.

"Here he comes, now," Meg said.

"Who? Arne Chenoweth?"

She nodded. "He's the biggest of the two men in front."

Rock studied the approaching riders. Chenoweth was big, broad shouldered, heavy. He held his body erect, glancing from side to side as he came down the street. He waved to the men on the porch of the store as he passed it. The man riding next to him was lean and seemed to hunch wearily in his saddle. Near the sheriff's office, Chenoweth turned and spoke to those behind him, then pulled into the tie-rail. His men continued down the street to the Golden Horseshoe saloon.

"Good morning, Meg," Chenoweth said, pulling off his hat. "I hoped I'd find you in town when I got here."

"Father and I rode in with Mr. Wesley," Meg said.

Chenoweth glanced at Rock, and nodded. He had sharp, dark eyes which were neither friendly nor unfriendly.

"Mr. Wesley has a horse ranch near Sawtelle," Meg continued. "He was driving some brood mares across country when he was ambushed, north of our ranch."

Chenoweth's face darkened. "The Temple Hills crowd, huh? I've said for a year, now, that we ought to get together and drive the outlaws out of those hills. We've put it off too long. Did they get your horses, Wesley?"

Rock nodded. "And two of my men."

"You've reported it to the sheriff?"

"Just a few minutes ago."

"What did he say?"

"That he'd head a posse that way tomorrow."

"Good," Chenoweth nodded. "Some of my men will go along. I will, too, if I can make it. Maybe we'll have better luck this time than we've had before."

"I hope so, too," Rock said, matching Chenoweth's aloof friendliness. "We had a little trouble with rustlers, ourselves, up near Sawtelle about a year ago."

"That so?" Chenoweth asked.

"Yep. One rancher after another suffered losses, and somehow or other, the rustling got blamed on a band from the Piutes. Only, there weren't any rustlers in the Piutes. The men responsible for the rustling were two of the ranchers who had been doing the most howling about the losses they had suffered."

The friendly look faded from Chenoweth's eyes. He leaned forward. "Now, what the hell do you mean by that?"

"I was just mentioning what happened near Sawtelle," Rock said smiling. "Why? What did I say that was wrong?"

Chenoweth took a deep breath. For a moment longer he stared at Rock, his eyes hard and unblinking. Then he looked at Meg, and his expression changed, a pleasant smile coming back to his lips.

"Don't disappear too quickly," he begged. "I have to see a man, then I want to talk to you."

"I'll probably be on the hotel porch," Meg said.

Chenoweth reined his horse away and continued on down the street, and Meg looked at Rock.

"You almost said too much," she told him bluntly.

Rock shrugged. He asked, "Meg, what do you think? Is there an outlaw band in the Temple Hills?"

"There could be," Meg said.

"What do you really think?"

She faced him defiantly. "I think you're not going to live very long, unless you're more careful."

He turned and stared at Chenoweth, who had pulled up in front of the Golden Horseshoe and was dismounting. As far as he had been able to tell, Chenoweth indicated no guilty knowledge of what had happened north of the McAlpin ranch, but that, in itself, meant nothing. He wondered abruptly at the man's interest in Meg McAlpin and grew aware that she was speaking to him.

"Do you want to walk to the hotel with me, Mr. Wesley?"

He nodded, smiled, and they turned up the street together.

4

Arne Chenoweth was caught in the grip of a driving anger, but he held it under a tight control as he rode to the Golden Horseshoe and pulled up in front of it. He dismounted, tied his horse among others at the hitch-rack, crossed the boardwalk to the saloon and strode inside.

The men who had come to town with him were at the bar, drinking and laughing over something one of them had said. He walked forward, pushed into the narrow space between Ollie Reed and Dutch Wyman, widening it with an aggressive thrust of his shoulders. He looked at Reed, then Wyman, then settled on Reed, who officially was his foreman at the ranch, a grade above Wyman in importance.

"Did you see who was in front of the sheriff's office?" he asked bluntly.

"Meg McAlpin and some stranger," Reed answered.

"No, it was Meg and one of the three men who were cutting across the country north and east of here with the Morgan mares."

Reed straightened. He was tall, thin, gaunt, and in his late forties. He had a brown, deeply wrinkled face and a long, hooked nose.

"You could be wrong, Arne," he said softly.

"The hell!" Chenoweth snapped. "I thought you told me all three men were killed."

"They were."

"I say you're lying. One got away. How?"

Ollie Reed moistened his lips. He looked suddenly uncomfortable. "We buried two," he said slowly. "The third fell over his horse but hung in the saddle. He had two bullets through him, one through the chest, one through the head. And his horse was creased by a bullet. It ran away. We chased it into the trees and finally caught it, but the man who had been riding it had dropped from the saddle."

"Alive—"

"Arne, we were sure he was dead. We looked for him, but—"

"Why in hell didn't you look until you found him?"

"We wanted to get away with the Morgans in case McAlpin or his men heard the shooting and came up to investigate. Besides, we were sure he was dead. Like I told you, I fired the shot that got him through the chest. At the same time, Dutch hit him in the head."

"You both missed," Chenoweth said flatly. "At least, he's still living. And he's told his story to McAlpin, and the sheriff, and God knows how many more. Tomorrow morning Sale is leading a posse north."

"After the Temple Hill outlaws?" Reed asked dryly. "They'll never find them."

"What kind of trail will they find to follow?"

"None, after a few miles. We blotted it with a herd of our cattle."

Chenoweth reached for one of the bottles on the bar. He asked for a glass and poured a drink. He had another. Ordinarily he didn't drink until late afternoon, but this morning he needed something to dull the anger he was feeling.

"I can't figure how the man got away," Dutch Wyman said. "But if I missed him the other day, I won't miss him the next time."

Chenoweth shook his head. "To kill him now—without any reason—"

"I'll have a reason," Wyman growled.

Chenoweth glanced at him. Wyman was a short, chunky man with one of the ugliest faces he ever had seen. His bulk made him look awkward, but he wasn't awkward when it came to guns. He was one of the fastest men in the country.

"We don't really have a hell of a lot to worry about," Ollie Reed said thoughtfully. "Sale's posse won't find anything when they go chasing after the Temple Hills outlaws, and if this man who got away runs into trouble, and gets himself killed, who's going to push any hunt for the Morgans? Later we can fake our own drive to Winslow—we come back with some Morgans. Who'll know the difference?"

Chenoweth had a third drink. Anger still pushed at him, but he was beginning to feel a little better. Ollie and he had worked a long time together—and there had been mistakes before, but they had always worked them out. When he had first heard of the Morgans, he had known he had to have them. And now, having them, he would keep them. There were few things he loved more than horses.

He glanced at Dutch Wyman. He said, "Nothing too open, Dutch."

"I'll kill him on Main Street," Dutch said. "But no one will blame me—I'll promise you that."

Chenoweth nodded crisply. He turned away, stepped outside, and looked up and down the street. There were a few more people on the street, a few more horses at the tie-rails. He remembered Meg had said she would be waiting for her father on the hotel porch and he could see her there, but right now he needed a more direct release—Meg had been playing too hard to get.

Thank God, every woman wasn't like that. Take Edna Bradley, for instance.

He got to thinking of Edna and felt the sudden need to see her, in spite of the fact that someone might see him if he went there in the daytime. A thing like that could be explained, though. If he ever was asked he could say he wanted to get her to make new curtains for his ranch house. Edna occasionally did sewing for others to supplement the small income her husband made as a bartender at the Long Chance saloon.

He cut across the street, angling in the direction of Edna Bradley's.

She looked startled when she answered his knock and saw him on the porch. She gasped, "Arne! What are you doing here at this hour?"

He laughed, stepped inside, closed the door and took her in his arms. That she was flustered and fought with him a little, only made it better. She was a big woman, hard-muscled, but she could be soft and pliable, too, and she didn't fight very long.

There was no danger that Frank Bradley would walk in. His work at the saloon kept him away from home from midmorning until late at night.

Rock Wesley signed for a room at the hotel, left Meg in the lobby and walked on up the street. He came to the Long Chance saloon, entered it, and at the bar ordered a drink he really didn't want. There were no other customers. He and the tall, thin, scowling man back of the bar had the place to themselves. The man back of the bar was named Frank Bradley.

"This another one of Chenoweth's places?" Rock asked, toying with his drink.

Bradley shook his head. "Nope. But I reckon he'll buy it some day. Right now, a man named Spencer owns it." He took a swipe at the bar top, looked at Rock and asked, "Stranger here?"

"Yep. What sort of man is Chenoweth?"

"Folks around here don't talk about him—unless they can say something nice."

"Do you talk about him?"

"No." Bradley's scowl deepened. He leaned across the bar, looking hard at Rock. "Just who are you, mister?"

"I'm a man who was driving some horses across country north of here and lost them to outlaws," Rock said. "I hear there're outlaws in the Temple Hills."

"You've lost your horses for good, mister," Bradley said.

"To outlaws?"

Bradley ignored him for the moment. After a while he said, "I ain't gonna tell you a thing, mister—except this. If my wife would leave this town, I'd get out tomorrow, but we've got a son buried here and she don't want to move away. So I've got to stay—but you better ride out."

"Forget my horses—and the Temple Hills outlaws?" Rock asked.

"You've lost your horses—I ain't saying more." Bradley turned away.

"Take another look at me, Bradley," Rock said very softly. "I'm not riding out. If I'm staying, who do I talk to?"

Bradley moistened his lips. "You might talk

to Roy Seigel, that is—if you're interested in buying land in the Modoc valley."

"Who's Roy Seigel?"

"He's an attorney up the street. His name is on his office window."

Rock nodded, paid for his drink, left the saloon, and walked on to Seigel's office. The door stood open. He looked inside. A girl was seated at one of the two desks in the room. She was wearing a light, summery dress, and had honey-colored hair and blue eyes.

She smiled at him and called, "Come on in. Roy isn't here right now but he should be back pretty soon. He's never gone very long."

Rock stepped in. "I'm Rock Wesley."

"Jinny Blake. You're new here. Looking for work?"

"No. I was driving some horses across country, north of here, when I ran into an ambush and lost them. I came in to report what had happened to the sheriff."

Jinny's face sobered. Her eyes went to the bandage around his head. She came slowly to her feet. "The Temple Hills outlaws?"

"That's what the sheriff said."

"Did you see any of them?"

"No."

Jinny's lips tightened. "No one ever does. What's Henry Sale going to do?"

"Lead a posse north, tomorrow morning."

She looked at him, and there was a sudden caution, a hint of worry, behind the blue eyes. "I'm sorry you lost your horses, Mr. Wesley. What did you want to see Roy Seigel about?"

Rock grinned. "Some law business. I'd rather talk to him about it."

"I see." She stood up, reached for a jacket hanging on a wall. "I've got to step out a moment, Mr. Wesley. You can wait here." She stopped at the door, and looked back. She was slender, and had a nice figure. She said slowly, "I think you're wise to talk to Roy Seigel about—whatever you want to talk to him about."

She left. Rock grinned, took one of the chairs in the room, and sat waiting for Roy Seigel. He didn't have long to wait. In less than five minutes, Seigel appeared. The attorney was a tall, gaunt, hungry-looking man who might have been about forty years old. He was slightly stooped. His coat hung on him like a sack. He had a bony face, thin, colorless lips, a long straight nose and deep-set, watery eyes. He said, "Hello, Wesley. I met Jinny down the street. She said I'd find you here."

"Did she tell you what I wanted?" Rock asked.

"No, but she told me what you said. Do you want to know what you ought to do?"

"Yes."

"Fork your horse and ride, and don't waste any time about it."

"Why?"

"Because the horses you lost are gone. The posse which will leave here tomorrow won't find any trace of them—or of the outlaws who are supposed to have taken them."

"And if I stay around and hunt for them closer to Modoc?"

"You'll run into an argument, Wesley. It will end up in a gunfight, and a funeral. Your funeral."

Rock could feel himself getting angry. He stared at Seigel. "Do you know what you're telling me? You're telling me that there are no outlaws in the hills. You're telling me that Chenoweth took my mares, and that there's nothing I can do about it. Two men were murdered in the ambush the other day. They were as close to me as brothers. I can't do anything about that, either, can I? What kind of a town is this?"

Seigel shrugged. He walked to his desk and sat down. "It's a frightened town, Wesley. A gutless town. Say whatever you want to about it, and you won't be telling half the truth. We've had a few heroes but they never lasted very long."

"And how long do you expect to last if you talk to others as you have to me?"

A wry smile twisted the attorney's lips. "You're a marked man, Wesley. If you run, no harm's been done by what I've said. If you don't run, you're finished."

"So it's as simple as that."

"Exactly."

Rock took a deep breath. He stopped at the door and stood there, staring into the street. A voice in his mind was telling him to listen to what Seigel had said, to take his loss and forget it, to fork his horse and get out of town. No other course was sensible.

He glanced back at the attorney. Seigel had taken a bottle from one of the drawers of his desk and had poured out a stiff drink. He tossed it off, and poured another. "Whiskey numbs a person's sensitivity," he said bleakly. "If I take enough, I can live with myself. Why the hell did you have to come here and make it harder?"

"There'll be others, after me," Rock said. "How much whiskey can you carry?"

He didn't wait for an answer. He stepped outside and turned down the street.

Meg McAlpin watched him from the porch of the hotel. She expected him to notice her and was ready to wave when he did, but he didn't look toward the hotel. Then, as she saw he was nearing the Golden Horseshoe saloon and saw the four men standing in front of it, she came quickly to her feet, her hands suddenly clenched, her breath coming faster. She felt an impulse to hurry after him and stop him, but by this time it was too late. A tight, dry pain gripped her throat.

Jinny Blake also watched him. She had been smiling, but her smile disappeared abruptly. The stranger whom she had met in Roy Seigel's office had reached the corner of the Golden Horseshoe saloon, had stopped there and stood facing Ollie Reed, Jake Layden, Abe Roebuck and Dutch Wyman. Vaguely she realized that she had been about to go somewhere, do something—whatever she had been about to do was completely wiped from her mind.

The sheriff, also, was watching the scene in front of the Golden Horseshoe. He stood in his office doorway, scowling, aware of a mixture of emotions. Running through his mind was the thought that it possibly wasn't going to be necessary to make the long, hard ride into the Temple Hills in the morning; but over and above this lay a feeling of uneasiness at what was about to happen. He knew that as the sheriff, he ought to do something about it. He also knew he wasn't expected to, and that Chenoweth would resent it if he interfered, which wasn't right. As sheriff, he was entitled to more attention and consideration than he was getting.

Rock Wesley was unaware that anyone was interested in where he was going. He had no particular destination in mind. He was still upset and angry as a result of his talk with Roy Seigel. He knew he wasn't going to run, but he had no idea at all of how he was going to handle the problem he faced.

He passed several buildings, then, at the corner of the Golden Horseshoe saloon, he came to an abrupt stop. Four men stood on the saloon porch, four who had ridden into town with Chenoweth, and all were staring at him. But that wasn't what had stopped him. His attention was caught by a bridle one of the men was holding—a silver-studded bridle made of soft, plaited leather. Rock knew that bridle better than his own. It had belonged to Stu Henley. It had been on the horse Stu had been riding the day of the ambush.

He looked at the man holding it—a short, chunky man with small, pale blue eyes, a crooked nose, and thick, coarse lips. He glanced at the others. All four were tense. All four were waiting rigidly to see what he would do. They had understood he would recognize the bridle and appreciate its significance. They were expecting to be challenged.

Rock pushed back his hat. He felt strangely calm. He knew that he had two choices. He could back down, turn away, and maybe if he did he might make it across the street to where his horse was tied and be able to get out of town—and run. Or he could start asking questions, and die. Against four men, he had no chance at all.

"Like the bridle, mister?" said the man holding it.

Rock nodded. "Yes. Where did you get it?"

"From the horse of a man who won't need it any more."

"Are you the one who killed him?"

"Could be."

"Where did your bullet hit him?"

"Right through the head."

"Then that's where I'll shoot you," Rock said. "You can reach for your gun any time, mister. But when you reach for it, reach fast."

He was leaning a little forward, the weight of his body resting on the balls of his feet. His arms hung at his side, slightly bent at the elbows. He was watching the man with the bridle, but was equally aware of the others. They were too tightly grouped, and seemed to realize it. The two nearest the street stepped farther that way. The one close to the building edged up against it. The one with the bridle had started crouching over. His right hand was poised inches above his gun, his fingers curved like claws.

Rock waited quietly, checking off the seconds. The man holding the bridle dropped it, and with his other hand, grabbed for his gun.

Rock's hand swept back to his holster. He snapped his first shot the instant his gun was free. He did not get Wyman in the head, as he had promised. There had been no time to raise his gun enough. His bullet, instead, ripped into the man's chest and the force of it was driving him backward, and off balance. Rock fired again, this time at the man to Wyman's left who had drawn his gun and who was screaming at the others. He threw a shot at the man nearest the building, then threw himself toward the corner of the building in a stumbling dive.

A shot whistled past him as he fell, another burned his upper arm. He scrambled to his knees, saw one of the men ducking between the rearing horses at the tie-rail and another lying prone on the boardwalk, motionless. He fired at the man ducking between the horses, but fired too high. The man on the boardwalk made an effort to get up, but fell again. He couldn't see what had happened to the man who had been holding the bridle, or the one who had been nearest the saloon.

Still on his knees, he broke and reloaded his gun, and a moment later saw the sheriff hurrying toward him from across the street. The sheriff was waving a gun in the air and was shouting, "That's all! That's all! There'll be no more shooting!"

Rock stood up, but didn't leave the protection of the corner of the building. He was beginning to feel a little shaky. There was a stinging pain in his arm where a bullet had scraped him, but otherwise he was unhurt. He holstered his gun, mopped a hand over his face and took a long, deep breath. He thought he could understand why he still was living. Those whom he had faced in front of the saloon had depended too much on one man. When the other three had decided to take a hand, it had been too late. Next time—if there was a next time—they would take no chances. That was something to keep in mind.

A crowd was gathering. The sheriff knelt briefly at the side of Dutch Wyman, then at the side of the other man. After that, he stepped toward Rock Wesley.

"I'll take your gun, Wesley," he said gruffly.

"Why? I didn't start it. I just defended myself."

"That's right," someone agreed. "I saw what happened from in front of the feed store. Since when do we arrest a man for self-defense?"

The sheriff glanced at the one who had spoken, a thin young man with rusty hair and a splash of freckles across his cheeks. "Keep out of this, Fleming," he said angrily.

"Ask someone else what happened," Fleming said stubbornly. "There were plenty who saw it."

Others in the crowd were nodding in an apparent agreement with Fleming. An indecisive look came into the sheriff's eyes.

"I'll be around if you want me," Rock offered. "I'm not going any place."

The sheriff gnawed at his lips. This was a serious problem to him. Wesley had shot down two of Chenoweth's men. Chenoweth was not going to like it if the stranger went free. Then it struck the sheriff that it might be a smart thing not to arrest the stranger. A man in jail was entitled to protection.

"All right," he agreed. "But don't leave town, Wesley. Don't try to get away."

"Thanks," Rock said dryly.

He pushed his way through the crowd and started down the street, and almost immediately was joined by Roy Seigel.

"I've an idea you could stand a drink," Seigel said. "And I know where they serve the best liquor in Modoc."

"Where?"

"My office."

"Then let's go there," Rock said.

5

It was late afternoon. Rock was still in Roy Seigel's office, leaning back in one chair, his feet in another. On the desk near him was a cup of coffee. After two drinks and a long session devoted to talking, Seigel had insisted that they switch to coffee, which he had brewed on a stove in his living quarters, a room back of the office.

Jim Fleming came in.

"Where is he?" Seigel asked.

"At the Golden Horseshoe," Jim answered. "He showed up on the street about half an hour ago, went to the Golden Horseshoe where he probably heard what happened. Then he went to see the sheriff. He was with Henry Sale for maybe twenty minutes. After that he walked on back to the saloon."

"How did he look?"

"Angry."

Seigel laughed. He said, "Pour yourself some coffee in the back room."

Fleming walked that way. He had joined Rock Wesley and Seigel here shortly after their arrival, but an hour ago had gone out to see if Arne Chenoweth was in town and where he could be found. While he was gone, Seigel had characterized him to Rock as a young man who had not yet found himself. He had a ranch to the south and east of Modoc, more or less out of the way of direct conflict with Chenoweth. He lived there alone, occasionally had a hired hand to help him. He was unmarried. He once had been in love with Jinny Blake, but now seemed interested in Meg McAlpin. "But he won't go far in that direction," Seigel said. "Meg just isn't interested in getting married to anyone."

Jinny Blake showed up in the street doorway. "Can I come in?"

"Come ahead," Seigel invited. "Enter the cave of Adullam."

"The cave of Adullam?" Jinny repeated.

"Don't you read your Bible?" Seigel asked. "The cave of Adullam was the place where David took refuge after he had been outlawed by King Saul. It was a gathering place for the discontented. Are you discontented?"

"Yes."

"Then this is where you belong."

Rock took his feet off the chair. Jinny appropriated the seat.

Jim came in from the back room with a cup of coffee, noticed Jinny, and came to an abrupt stop. It was hard to tell which of the two was most surprised.

"Jim, give Jinny your coffee," Seigel said. "Pour more for yourself."

"Sure," Jim said.

He stepped forward, gave Jinny the coffee, and returned for more. When he came back, he stood behind Seigel's chair, and was very careful not to look at Jinny.

"What are you planning?" Jinny asked.

"Nothing very startling," Rock said. "I want to have a talk with Arne Chenoweth."

Jinny stood up. She looked worried. "Any way you figure it," she said slowly, "Arne Chenoweth is Arne Chenoweth, and this is Modoc, and the deaths of Dutch Wyman and Ollie Reed only make matters worse. What you ought to be doing is planning how to get Mr. Wesley safely out of town."

"But I'm not ready to go," Rock said. "I doubt I could make it anyhow."

He crossed to the window and stood there, staring into the street. His nerves were steady again. He knew that what had happened in front of the Golden Horseshoe saloon had made him a marked man here in the Modoc Valley, but there was nothing he could do about that. Nor had Seigel offered him much hope in their talk this afternoon. The attorney had admitted that there were a number of ranchers in the valley who might have reason to join in a revolt against Chenoweth, but he doubted that any had the courage to jump into a hopeless fight.

"When do you want to have your talk with Chenoweth?" Seigel asked.

"Why put it off?" Rock answered.

Seigel got to his feet. "Then give Jim and me about ten minutes to set the stage."

"Ten minutes," Rock agreed.

He watched the two leave the office, then turned to Jinny.

"What are they going to do?" Jinny asked.

"They're going to get some men over to the Golden Horseshoe—men who might be considered impartial witnesses."

"And then what?"

"Then I'm going to say a few things to Arne Chenoweth."

"You think he'll listen?"

"Maybe not, but when you get shoved into as narrow a corner as the one I'm in, you'll try anything."

This seemed to make sense to the girl. She nodded, walked to the door and looked out, then turned to face him. "How did Jim Fleming happen to get mixed up in this?" she asked bluntly.

"It was Jim who challenged the sheriff in front of the saloon when he wanted to arrest me."

"Jim did that?"

"Yes. Later, he joined us here."

A strange look crossed Jinny's face. She was silent for a moment, then said, "Mr. Wesley, I don't know what you hope to accomplish by talking to Arne Chenoweth, but I wish you luck."

"Thanks, Jinny," Rock said.

He watched her leave the office and angle across the street toward the store. A few minutes later he started for the Golden Horseshoe.

Arne Chenoweth sat at his regular table. He had been drinking, but not heavily. Four men sat with him, waiting for what he had to say.

Finally he centered his attention on Abe Roebuck. "What happened to the bridle?" he asked sharply.

Roebuck, a thin, middle-aged man, shook his head. "I don't know, Arne. I ducked back here after Wesley made for the corner of the building. I meant to go out the back door and cut him off in the alley, but before I could, the sheriff was there, and a mob. Maybe the sheriff got the bridle."

"He didn't," Chenoweth said. "I asked him. Why the hell did Dutch use the bridle?"

"He was sure it would make Wesley jump him."

"Did his gun stick in its holster?"

Abe Roebuck shook his head. "Nope. Wesley was faster. I never saw anyone pull a gun fast as he did."

Chenoweth looked at Tom Garmish. "You agree, Tom?"

"He was fast, all right," Garmish nodded. "But if Reed hadn't come between us—"

"What happened to the bridle?"

"Dutch dropped it. I don't know who picked it up."

Chenoweth poured another drink. A damned bunch of fools, and this time he had no Ollie Reed to help him think his way out of a situation. By now Wesley would have told a number of people about the bridle he had identified. Of course, he could prove nothing, but there were always people willing to believe something like that, proof or no. Wesley hadn't picked up the bridle—but it had definitely been a mistake to use it. The bridle was incriminating. Who had it now—who?

The street door opened and two men came in, Roy Seigel and the sheriff. They headed for the bar. Chenoweth's eyes narrowed. He knew that Seigel had no use for the sheriff and that Henry Sale wasn't overly fond of the attorney. It struck him as rather strange that they should be together. Three more men came in, Fleming and two ranchers from the hills to the east. They also angled toward the bar.

Chenoweth watched them, aware of a growing uneasiness. Four others came in, four men from town. Chenoweth recognized no friends among them, or even constant patrons of his saloon.

"What about Wesley?" Garmish asked. "You want us to take care of him here in town or wait until he rides out somewhere?"

"Not in town," Chenoweth said. He began to curse, then broke off.

Another man had come in from the street—

Wesley. Chenoweth's eyes narrowed. A warning flashed through his mind. There was nothing accidental about Wesley's coming here, or about the presence of the men from town, of the sheriff and Roy Seigel, and the three ranchers. Whatever was going to happen had been planned. An icy chill ran over his body—he felt like a fighter off-balance, and the experience wasn't pleasant. He moistened his lips, tried to make himself relax. He saw that Garmish had reached for his gun, and said under his breath, "Not here, Garmish. Put it away."

Then he waited for Wesley to come to him.

Rock Wesley moved directly across the room toward Chenoweth. Two of Chenoweth's men were facing him as he came in. The others turned as he drew near, and he could sense the tension which gripped them. He was aware of something else, too. The room had grown quiet. Those at the bar and at the other tables were watching him.

"Hello, Chenoweth," he said abruptly.

"Pull up a chair and sit down," Chenoweth invited.

He shook his head. "I want to ask some questions. Do you know where my horses are?"

Chenoweth's face got red. His lips worked, but with an obvious effort he managed to keep his anger under control. "No, I don't. I don't even know that you had any horses, or that you lost them as you said you did."

"I had the horses," Rock answered. "And I lost them exactly the way I told the sheriff. But the reason I'm here is this. One of your men, Dutch Wyman, had a bridle in his hand this morning. It was a plaited bridle with silver mountings. He boasted that he took it from the horse of a man who didn't need it any more. That man was Stu Henley, who worked for me. His horse was wearing that bridle when he was shot down in the ambush."

Chenoweth made a sweeping motion with his arm. "I don't know anything about any bridle, and Dutch isn't here to defend himself. All I can tell you is this. No man working for me had anything to do with your ambush. I don't know where your horses are, and I don't know whether I care or not."

"But I do," Rock said slowly. "I'm going to find out what happened to them, and I'm going to find out who killed my men."

"Go right ahead. Seems to me you've got a couple of killings hanging over you, as of today."

"Self-defense," Rock said. "You worry on this—fifteen mares are hard to hide."

Arne Chenoweth jerked to his feet. He had taken about all he could. He asked hoarsely, "Are you calling me a rustler?"

"Are you one?"

"No, by God."

"Then you don't have anything to worry about—but call your men off my back, Chenoweth, or more of them are going to get hurt. And pass the word along—I'm interested in buying that bridle one of your men had this morning."

Chenoweth said, "I'll pass the word along. But I don't know anything about any bridle."

"Two men at your table do." Rock pointed at Garmish and Abe Roebuck.

Chenoweth glanced at the two men. He said, "Garmish, what's this about a bridle?"

"I didn't see any bridle," Garmish answered promptly.

"You lie," Rock snapped. "You heard every word that was said this morning. You saw the bridle in Dutch Wyman's hand."

Garmish came slowly to his feet. His breath made a hissing sound as he pulled it in. A sudden perspiration showed on his forehead and around his lips. His right hand was close to his holstered gun. He shook his head from side to side. "No man can call me a liar, Wesley," he cried hoarsely. "I tell you, Dutch didn't have a bridle in his hand."

Henry Sale showed a flare of courage. He left the bar, stepped toward Chenoweth's table. He drew his gun, "That's enough, Garmish," he shouted. "Enough from you, too, Wesley. I'll drop the first man to reach for his gun."

Chenoweth looked around irritably. "Wesley asked for it."

"But there'll be no shooting," Sale rumbled.

Garmish looked relieved. He reached for the bottle on the table and poured a drink.

Rock shrugged. He turned abruptly on his heel and headed for the door. His back muscles were tensed against the possible shock of a bullet, and he half expected to hear a shout of warning from someone. But nothing like that happened. He reached the door, opened it, stepped outside, and let it swing shut behind him.

6

Roy Seigel paced back and forth across his office, now and then slapping his fist into the palm of his hand and laughing. "I never saw anything like it," he declared. "Neither has anyone else in this town. Once, at least, Arne Chenoweth got more shoveled on him that he could shovel back."

Rock, standing at the window and staring into the street, said nothing. He noticed Fleming talking to Jinny on the porch of the store. He saw three men ride by, leaving town, and saw two others ride in. Meg McAlpin, who had been on the hotel porch during much of the afternoon, was gone. He supposed she and her father were on their way home.

"Chenoweth's facing a problem right now," Seigel said. "He can't take a thing like this lying down. It might give other men ideas. He's got to put you in your place, but he can't be too crude about it. I wish we knew what happened to that bridle."

"I looked for it after the shooting was over," Rock said. "But there was a crowd by then and the bridle wasn't where Dutch Wyman had dropped it."

"I suppose one of Chenoweth's men got it."

"Maybe."

"Too bad. We could have nailed them with it, if we could have proved Dutch Wyman really had it. What are you planning next?"

"I'll ride out with the posse in the morning."

"You'll be wasting a day, but I suppose it can't be helped."

Rock swung around to face the attorney. He said, "Seigel, where will I find my mares?"

"Somewhere on Chenoweth's Arrowhead ranch."

"How will I find them?"

The attorney's face sobered. He shook his head. "I can't answer that. The Arrowhead takes in a lot of ground. Start searching it, and you're liable never to come back. Wherever the mares are, they'll be well guarded. If you get near the place you'll run into a bullet. You may run into one sooner."

"I may run into one when I step out on the street," Rock said.

He took another look through the window. Fleming had left Jinny and was heading this way. He stepped to the door and opened it.

"Chenoweth and his men still are in town," Fleming said as he came in. "Garmish was about half drunk when I left the Golden Horseshoe."

"Tell me about Garmish," Rock said.

"He's one of Chenoweth's riders, been here several years. He's quarrelsome, good with his fists and good with a gun."

"Then if he jumps me it won't be anything unusual?"

"Not at all."

"Chenoweth could take a chance on it, and not lose a thing?"

"Exactly."

"So I might have a fight on my hands?"

"If you run into Tom Garmish tonight it's almost a sure bet that you will."

Rock crossed to one of the chairs in the room and sat down. He had run a bluff in the Golden Horseshoe saloon a little while ago, but a bluff wouldn't help him recover his horses or bring Chenoweth to justice. He could count on no help from the sheriff.

Fleming stepped forward, "I can sort of keep an eye on Garmish for you, if you want me to," he offered.

"No reason for you to get mixed up in this," Rock said. "Or you either, Seigel."

"Chenoweth already knows where I stand," Seigel said.

Rock shook his head. A sudden restlessness gripped him. He got up and strode to the door.

"Where are you going?" Seigel asked.

"I want to see the sheriff again. Then I'm going to stable my horse and have supper."

"I usually eat in the Silver Grill."

"Then I may see you there."

"I may be there, too," Fleming said.

Rock nodded, and stepped outside. The sun was down and night was thickening in the sky. He turned down the street to the sheriff's office, but the sheriff wasn't there. The horse he had borrowed from McAlpin was still at the tie-rail. He unlooped the reins and led the animal down to the livery stable at the end of Main Street. On the way back he met Meg McAlpin. She was walking toward him, her head lowered as though in thought. He waited until she was quite near, then said, "Hello, Meg. I thought you'd be home by now."

She looked up, startled, and didn't smile as he had thought she would. Instead, that frown he was coming to recognize showed on her face, and her lips tightened. "What are you doing up here at this end of town, alone?" she asked slowly. "Don't you know that Arne Chenoweth's men still are here?"

"And where would I be safe?" Rock asked.

Meg bit her lips. "Are fifteen horses worth it?"

"Worth what?"

"Worth dying—and killing for?"

Rock shook his head. "Maybe not. But if I had been killed in the ambush and if Stu Henley and Vic Anderson had escaped, they'd be here, doing what I'm doing."

"Throwing their lives away."

"I might live through it."

"No. You were lucky this morning. And you

were lucky in the saloon, if what I heard was correct. But the next time Arne Chenoweth makes a move, you may not be lucky."

"So I'll get hurt. But a man does what he has to do, Meg. There's no help for it. You can't run away from the problems life dishes up."

"But you don't have to be reckless about it. You didn't have to come up here alone."

"I had to stable the horse your father let me use."

The girl made a weary movement with her shoulders. She came a step closer. "I decided to stay over with my married sister. She lives near here."

"Let me walk you there."

"No. You're going to walk me back to the hotel, or the restaurant, or the Long Chance saloon. You'll be safer there than on the street."

"Safe because you're with me?"

"Yes. And don't be foolish about it. I know Arne Chenoweth better than you do. His men, too."

"If they're as bad as that, why do you put up with them in Modoc?"

"We haven't had much choice."

"People always have a choice," Rock said.

"Where do you want to go?" she asked.

"The Silver Grill restaurant," Rock said. "And some day I'd like you to have supper with me there."

She gave him a strange look. "Some day, maybe I will."

"Next night we're both in town?"

"Maybe."

They came to the restaurant and stopped briefly in front of it. There, Rock turned to face her. He said, "Thanks, Meg."

She nodded. "I can't make you be careful, can I? There isn't anything I can say that will make you change your mind about what you're doing?"

"No, Meg. There isn't."

She put out her hand. "Be careful, anyhow. Don't take any chances you don't have to."

"I can promise that, anyhow," Rock agreed.

She shook hands like a man, her clasp warm and firm. Then she turned swiftly and walked back down the street, hurrying.

Rock joined Roy Seigel at one of the tables at the side of the room. Two others were at the table, ranchers from the east hills, whom Seigel introduced as Sam Dobell and Lou Simmons. Both were middle-aged men. Neither had much to say.

Jim Fleming came in when Rock had eaten and was finishing his coffee. Jim leaned over and whispered, "Garmish is out front. He's not as drunk as he seems."

Rock nodded and glanced toward the door. "Thanks. What about the back way?"

"Could be someone back there, too," Fleming admitted.

"What's behind the restaurant? A yard?"

"You could call it that, but it's not fenced. Want me to get you a horse?"

"Not this time."

He finished his coffee and glanced at Seigel who was looking at him curiously, and doubtless wondering what Fleming had said.

"Had enough to eat?"

"More than enough."

They stood up, and Seigel moved closer to him.

"Garmish is out front," Rock said under his breath. "I'm leaving here the back way. Where will you be later on tonight?"

"At the Long Chance saloon," Seigel said. "Garmish might look for you there, but I doubt it. He wouldn't find many friends at the Long Chance. There might be someone back of the restaurant. Have you thought of that?"

"Even so, they expect me out front," Rock said.

He turned abruptly toward the door to the kitchen, pushed through it, and hurried toward the rear door. A woman at the stove looked around at him, startled, but said nothing. He drew his gun, hesitated momentarily, then opened the rear door. He stepped into the darkness beyond, moved swiftly to one side and dropped down on his knees. The shot he more than half expected did not come. His eyes probed the inky shadows, but he could detect no sign of movement. He listened, but heard no unusual sounds. After counting up to a full minute, he risked getting to his feet.

At the corner of the building, he stopped, then moved on, and a little while later holstered his gun, satisfied no one had been waiting for him back here.

He circled carefully to the rear of the hotel, found its back door locked. He moved to the front and, standing in shadow, studied the street. He could see no sign of Garmish or any other Chenoweth men he recognized. Finally he stepped up on the porch and crossed to the door.

The clerk who had rented him a room that morning looked surprised when he came in, but gave him his key without comment.

"I'm going to sleep," Rock said. "And I don't want to be disturbed. Understand?"

"Sure." Something stirred in the clerk's eyes, like the beginning of a tired joke, but he never uttered it.

Rock started down the corridor toward his room. He knew that his request for privacy would mean nothing to the clerk if Garmish or anyone else connected with Chenoweth decided to visit him tonight. But he didn't mean to stay here. He meant to lock his door, block it from the inside, then leave through the window. He had to meet Seigel at the Long Chance—he still had work to do tonight. He thought he could do it better if Chenoweth thought him safely out of the way.

He came to the door, unlocked it, and stepped inside. He had no warning at all that anyone was in the room waiting for him, other than a brief memory of the clerk's sly face, when the other had been about to make his joke, and then thought better of it. The heavy blow which smashed against the back of his head came soundlessly from the darkness.

It drove him to his knees, and while he sagged there, swaying and trying to fight off the numbing shock, someone struck a match and lit the lamp, and someone else closed and locked the door.

He looked up and saw two men, and heard a third behind him. One of the men he saw was Arne Chenoweth, scowling, hard-faced, with lips pulled back tightly against yellowing teeth. Chenoweth held a gun. The man standing beside Chenoweth was big and wide-shouldered. Rock didn't know him by name but had seen him at the table in the Golden Horseshoe with Chenoweth.

He came slowly to his feet. His legs felt shaky and the blow to his head had started his scalp wound hammering. His eyes didn't focus well.

"Hit him again, Abe," Chenoweth ordered.

Rock realized Chenoweth was talking to the man behind him. He lunged straight ahead, diving at Chenoweth. He felt a sharp blow on his shoulder, and as Chenoweth reeled backward from the force of his drive, the big man beside him took a hand. Rock felt himself swung toward the bed. He fell across it, rolled over, sat up and saw Abe Roebuck smashing a gun barrel at his head. He tried to duck away from the blow, but couldn't. It sliced against the side of his face like a knife.

Specks of light danced in front of his eyes. Someone pulled him erect. A fist ripped into his stomach, then smashed him squarely in the face as he was falling. He dropped across the bed again and heard it break. He tried to sit up, but couldn't. He now was only dimly aware of what was happening. His body had been gripped in a hammering sea of pain which was clouding his mind. He felt someone pulling at him, then heard Chenoweth say, "All right, let's see them." And a moment later he heard Chenoweth say, "Once more, Abe, but not too hard. The sheriff can finish him."

Abe Roebuck's gun barrel crashed down at his head once more, but he hardly felt the blow which knocked him unconscious.

Waking was a slow and painful process. The hammering in his head made it hard to think. He slid back several times into the shadows where the pain hardly could be felt, but after a time he had to stay aware of it, and live with it, and try to fight off the dizzy, sick feeling which held him.

The lamp in the room still was burning. The door was closed and he was alone. He could see a broken chair but he had no memory of how it had been broken. The bed was broken, but he had felt it break. And he was alive. That was the most puzzling thing of all. Why hadn't Chenoweth finished him? What did he stand to gain through letting him live?

After a time Rock was able to sit up. He touched the bandage over the wound in his scalp. It was moist with blood and the wound ached terribly. The left side of his face was raw. Blood from his nose had stained the front of his shirt. There was a mirror on the wall, but he didn't want to see what he looked like.

He glanced dully around the room. Surely the fight in here had been heard, but of course, no one had dared to interfere. And it was no problem to figure out how Chenoweth had gained access to the room. In Modoc, the word of Arne Chenoweth was law.

There were footsteps in the corridor outside. They stopped at his door. Someone knocked.

"Come in," he mumbled.

The door opened. The sheriff came in, a gun in his hand. He leveled the gun straight at Rock, and he snapped, "Stand up, Lafferty."

"Lafferty?" Rock said.

"Sure. Lafferty. Ringo Lafferty. You had me fooled for a while, but I've got it figured out now. You were in the crowd that rustled Rock Wesley's mares. You were badly wounded. When the McAlpins found you, you claimed you were Wesley. You knew if you gave your right name they would turn you over to the law."

Rock straightened a little. "You're wrong, sheriff. I've papers right here in my pocket to prove who I am. Letters, a bill of sale for the mares. Let me show you."

He reached into his pocket and drew out the papers he found there. He glanced at them, and caught his breath. These were not his papers—they were letters addressed to Ringo Lafferty at Roswell, New Mexico.

"All right, I'll take these," the sheriff said.

He leaned forward, jerked the letters out of Rock's hands, glanced at them and nodded with satisfaction. "Just as I thought." He stared grimly at Rock. "I'll take your gun now, mister."

Rock was beginning to understand now what had happened, why he had been attacked here in his room, and why he hadn't been killed. Chenoweth had had a better plan than murder. And when the posse rode out in the morning and found the bodies of Stu Henley and Vic Anderson, one of Chenoweth's riders doubtless would identify one of those bodies as Rock Wesley. And that would cinch the case. Ringo Lafferty was a well-known outlaw and rustler—notorious partly because no pictures of him were available for wanted circulars. He had never been caught. But no judge in the territory would waste much time in condemning a man proven to be Lafferty to be hanged.

Rock stood up, swaying uncertainly. "My name's not Lafferty," he insisted. "Give me a week and I can prove it."

"That's up to the judge, Lafferty," the sheriff said. He stepped back and to one side and motioned toward the door. "March—and don't try anything like resisting arrest. A lot of folks will breathe easier when you're dead."

7

Meg couldn't settle down that evening. She was tense, and found herself listening for the sound of shots that would tell her Rock Wesley was dead. It could end no other way.

Alice sensed how she felt, and was nervous herself. Her husband had gone back downtown after supper. She hadn't wanted him to because she too realized that there might be trouble in town, and sometimes, when there was shooting, an innocent bystander got hurt. She had quarreled with him about whether he should go or not, and that was another thing that bothered her. She did not like to quarrel with her husband.

Meg glanced at the clock. She walked to the front door, opened it and stared out into the night.

"I wouldn't do that if I were you," Alice called.

Meg looked around at her. "Why not? What's there to be afraid of here?"

"I just wouldn't do it—"

Meg closed the door. She moved slowly back to one of the chairs in the room, but didn't sit down.

"What's he like?" Alice asked.

"What's who like?"

"You know who I mean. This Rock Wesley."

Meg frowned. "He's like another man who

came here once, a man named Art Kellner."

"I don't think I remember him," Alice said.

"He wasn't here long. He had a quarrel with Dutch Wyman. There was a gunfight."

"Yes, I recall him now. He was killed, wasn't he?"

Meg nodded. She sat down. She was wondering why she had compared Rock Wesley with Art Kellner. They really weren't much alike in appearance or temperament, or probably in many other ways. Of course, she had known Kellner only briefly, and memory distorts things. The frown on her face grew deeper.

Alice was staring at her shrewdly. "You didn't fall in love with Wesley while he was out at the ranch, did you?"

"Of course not," Meg said quickly. "What in the world put that in your mind?"

"The way you're acting."

"And how should I act?" Meg cried. "A man is about to be killed for standing up for his rights. Am I supposed to like it?"

"Maybe you're not," Alice admitted. "But I still can't see why you have to get all broken up about it. I still can't see—"

She stopped speaking and looked quickly toward the door. Meg looked that way too, came to her feet and then relaxed as Fred Brady, Alice's husband, came in. He was young, pleasant looking, with dark hair and a round, chubby face.

He ran the feed store, which once had belonged to his father.

He crossed to where Alice was sitting, leaned over and kissed her, then waved a greeting to Meg. He asked, "What do you girls think's happened?" and there was a charge of excitement in his voice.

Meg's heart gave a jump. "How should we know?"

"That fellow who called himself Wesley wasn't Wesley at all. His real name is Ringo Lafferty, and he's a famous outlaw. I should have guessed it from the way he gunned down Ollie Reed and Dutch Wyman this morning. No ordinary rancher could handle a gun the way he did."

Meg felt as she once had, as a little girl, when her favorite horse had thrown her—she had landed with all the wind knocked out of her. She couldn't credit or grasp what she was hearing.

"I—don't understand," she said weakly.

"It's clear as anything could be," Brady said. "Ringo Lafferty was with the outlaws who killed Wesley and stole his mares, but he was badly wounded in the fight and the other outlaws left him to die. When you found him he told you his name was Wesley and that he was the one who had been ambushed. He had to have some way to explain his wound and he couldn't risk giving you his real name. Besides, he was pretty safe—

he's always been smart enough never to've had his picture taken."

Meg stiffened. "I don't believe it. I know he isn't Ringo Lafferty."

"I'm afraid he is, Meg. When the sheriff arrested him he found papers in his pocket, proving he was Ringo Lafferty."

"I saw those papers in his pocket," Meg declared angrily. "Father did too. There were a few letters addressed to him in Sawtelle, and a bill of sale for the mares. And the name was Rock Wesley, not Ringo Lafferty."

"That isn't what the sheriff says."

"Then the sheriff lies. And he could be lying. He takes his orders from Arne Chenoweth."

Brady was scowling. He said, "Meg, if you talk like that in town, you'll just get your father into trouble."

"But it's true, and you know it."

"It still isn't a smart thing to say."

"Who cares about that?"

"Your father might, Meg. He's not a young man any longer. It wouldn't be easy for him to start over again."

What Fred Brady was suggesting was so startling it frightened her. The McAlpin range bordered on Chenoweth's. It would be easy for Chenoweth to move in on the McAlpins. But she shook her head—until Fred mentioned it tonight, such a thing had never even been hinted.

In the meantime, another problem confronted her. Would her father want her to deny the papers they had seen in Rock Wesley's pocket? She didn't think so. She walked to the closet and got her jacket, and from there crossed to the door.

"Where are you going?" Brady asked.

"Out," Meg answered.

"But at this time of night—"

"What's wrong with this time of night?"

Alice called to her as she pulled open the door and stepped to the porch, but she made no reply. She walked swiftly through the darkness to Main Street, then up toward Roy Seigel's office. The office was dark, but a light showed from the back room. She knocked on the door until he answered.

"You, Meg?" he said, peering out at her. "What's happened?"

"Rock Wesley's been arrested."

"Yes, I know."

"They are claiming that he's really an outlaw named Lafferty."

"I know."

"Some papers were found in his pocket to prove it."

"That's what Henry Sale told me."

"But Roy, when father and I found him in the meadow, wounded, we looked at his papers. Everything he had on him identified him as Rock Wesley, of Sawtelle. There was a bill of sale for the mares, made out to Rock Wesley. There were letters addressed to him. He had no other papers, nothing with the name Lafferty on it."

"Papers can be switched, Meg."

"Then, that's what happened. What are we going to do about it?"

They had stepped inside the office and were standing in the dark. Seigel shook his head. "I don't know."

"Can't you wire someone in Sawtelle who could come here and identify him?"

"I doubt there's time. Unless I'm guessing wrong, Chenoweth already has sent someone to Centerville after the judge. He can make it here by day after tomorrow. The trial won't take fifteen minutes."

"Father and I can testify about the papers we found in his pocket. Would that do any good?"

"I don't know," Seigel said.

"But why wouldn't it?"

"Meg, I don't like to say this." Seigel sounded troubled. "Maybe your father won't want to testify. It would mean stepping right out in the open and defying Chenoweth. The last man who did anything like that got burned out."

She drew herself up proudly. "What kind of people do you think the McAlpins are?"

Seigel shrugged. "You've never bucked Chenoweth before—it might not help anyhow. Most people here like to think Chenoweth is right—

they could say your father was splitting proceeds with Lafferty's gang. Everybody knows Lafferty has friends among so-called 'honest' ranchers, though no one has been able to smoke them out."

Meg studied him intently. "Do you think my father would—consort with outlaws?"

Seigel smiled wearily. "I know he's never stood up to Chenoweth—and neither have you, Meg. Not even when Art Kellner was killed—" He held up a hand as Meg tried to interrupt. "I'm sorry, Meg, but I've made Chenoweth's business mine for a long time—besides, I don't blame you for being careful." Suddenly Seigel rested a hand lightly on Meg's shoulder. "Sleep on it Meg—there's nothing either of us can do tonight. At least you know it's Chenoweth we're up against, not one of his hirelings."

Meg's eyes were tense on Seigel's, hotly questioning. "Do you know Chenoweth ordered Art Kellner killed?"

Seigel shrugged again. "I know Dutch Wyman never took a breath that Chenoweth didn't approve. Dutch was ambitious—some day, I know, he hoped to ramrod Arrowhead—be Chenoweth's right-hand man. It's too late now to worry about Dutch Wyman—or Art Kellner. Wesley's still alive—and so is Chenoweth. It's time we chose sides."

Lightning flashed in the sky, momentarily brightening the almost deserted street. From far away came the rumbling sound of thunder. Meg shivered. She drew her jacket more closely around her.

"I've chosen sides, Roy," she whispered. "Just tell me what to do."

"Come in again tomorrow," Seigel suggested. "We'll figure something."

She nodded, and turned down the street toward her sister's home.

The rain woke her in the middle of the night. It still was raining in the morning and looked as though it would rain all day. At the breakfast table, Fred Brady announced that the posse, scheduled to ride north to the scene of the ambush, had put the trip off until the next day.

"I promised to ride with them," he explained. "But this storm was in the sky last night, and just before I came home, the sheriff said that if it rained, we wouldn't go. Henry doesn't like a wet ride."

Meg offered no comment. After the breakfast dishes had been cleared away and the baby had been fed, she stood for a time at the window, watching the rain. Someone hurried by in a slicker, toward town. This gave her an idea. It was a startling idea, but once it was in her mind she couldn't get rid of it.

After a time she looked into the kitchen. Alice was busy over a tub on a box, washing diapers.

Ordinarily, Meg would have offered to help, but this morning she didn't. Instead, she went to her sister's room. She knew that Fred kept a gun in the stand by the bed. She found it there, made sure it was loaded, and carried it to the spare room where she had slept. She hid it under the mattress. Then, in her jacket and with a towel over her head, she hurried out to the barn.

A slicker was rolled and tied behind her saddle. She freed it and put it on. It had two deep pockets. She went back to the house, and went immediately to her room. She put Roy's gun in one of the slicker pockets—it was heavier than she had thought, but with her hand in the pocket she didn't think the sag would show. When she came back to the front room, Alice was waiting for her, looking worried.

"Where in the world are you going, in all this rain?" she asked.

"I want to see Roy Seigel for a minute," Meg said untruthfully.

She opened the door, stepped outside, closed it and started hurrying through the rain toward the two-block business section. When she reached the main street she saw only three saddled horses standing at the tie-rails, and there was no one in sight. The rain was beginning to chill her. At the sheriff's office she stopped, and went inside.

Henry Sale sat at his desk, playing solitaire. He looked up when she came in, his eyes widening in surprise. His greeting was friendly enough but it was reserved, too, as though he half anticipated why she was here.

   She said, "I want to see Rock Wesley."

   Sale smiled. "His name isn't Wesley."

   "To me it is," Meg said. "I want to see him."

   The sheriff shook his head. "Sorry, you can't."

   Meg raised her voice. "Why not?"

   "No visitors."

   "And whose orders are those?"

   "Mine, Meg."

   "Then change them."

   "Sorry, Meg. I can't."

   Meg walked up to the desk. Her hands had been in her slicker pockets, one hiding the bulge of Fred Brady's gun, but she risked taking them out. She put them on the edge of the desk and leaned forward. "I want to see him, Henry," she said, and she was nearly screaming, now. "I've got to see him."

   Henry Sale looked flustered, but he shook his head. "Meg, be reasonable. The man's a dangerous outlaw."

   Meg raised her voice even higher. "Outlaw or not, I want to see him. Now, Henry! Right now!"

   "Now, Meg."

   She reached out and swept the cards off his desk. Two heavy stone paper-weights lay on some papers near her. She picked them up and hurled one at a picture on the wall. It broke the glass and knocked the picture to the floor. She hurled the other paper-weight at another picture, but missed. She knocked the papers the weights had been holding down to the floor. "Henry, I'm going to see him, and I'm going to see him now!" she screamed. "Do I have to go out somewhere and get a gun?"

The sheriff had jerked to his feet and backed away. He had never before seen Meg act like this, but it fell into a pattern he recognized. A woman sometimes went out of her head in anger when her man was arrested. A woman whose husband he had once arrested had grabbed a gun and tried to kill him.

Henry Sale put out his hand. "Now, wait a minute, Meg—" Sale glanced quickly at the door. He hoped no one would walk in on a scene like this. It would be as embarrassing to him as to Meg. He said again, "Now, wait a minute. You only want to see him?"

"I want to see that he's all right."

"If I let you see him, you'll stay only a minute?"

Sale turned, unlocked the door to the jail and walked down the corridor beyond. Meg followed him. She was shaky, now, and her face was flushed. She was ordinarily quiet, reserved—this was the first time in her life she had decided to let go—and it shocked her a little to discover how close to the surface of her play-acting real hysteria lay. But she was succeeding in what she had started to do, and that was the important thing. She put her right hand in the slicker pocket, over the gun.

The sheriff stopped at the second cell door. He called, "Lafferty, someone to see you," then stepped to one side.

Meg stopped. She saw someone move up to the iron grilled door and she heard Rock's voice growling. The sheriff was watching her sharply, almost suspiciously, and she knew what she had to do. The role she had been playing was only half finished. All she had accomplished could be ruined if she didn't carry it through as she had started.

She rushed forward to the cell door, her arms extended. She cried, "Rock—Rock!" And when she got to the door she thrust her arms through the bars and clutched his shoulders.

It was dark in the jail, but she could see that Rock's face was badly swollen on one side, and that she had startled him. She clutched him tighter, and whispered, "Act like this is real. Please."

"That won't be hard," he answered.

He stretched his arms through the bars to hug her, then spoke again, his voice very low. "I don't know what this is all about, but I approve of it."

Meg looked around at the sheriff. Her cheeks, now, were scarlet. She stamped her foot and cried, "Do you have to stand there watching? Haven't you any decency?"

Sale backed away a little, but didn't leave. And he wasn't going to leave. Meg suddenly was sure of that. She looked up at Rock's face in the shadows and spoke hurriedly, her voice low. "They won't let anyone in to see you. I buffaloed Henry—but he's likely to wake up any minute. They're going to rush your trial. I've brought you a gun. It's in my slicker pocket. I'll turn so that it's close to you. Get it while you can."

"Good girl," Rock said quietly.

Meg turned again so that her right side was to the bars in the door. She bowed her head as though crying. She covered her face with her arm and stayed that way until she felt Rock get the gun. Then she faced him once more.

"There's hardly anyone in town right now," she said hurriedly. "Later, this afternoon, men will ride in in spite of the rain. There's a horse tied just across the street. When you leave here, ride east."

"They'll know who brought me the gun," Rock said. "You're asking for trouble."

"That isn't important. You've got to get out so you can prove you're not Ringo Lafferty. No one else can prove it."

The sheriff stepped toward them. "That's enough, now," he said gruffly. "You've got to go, Meg."

She let her shoulders slump. She wondered if she was giving in too easily. She looked at Rock and said, "Nothing will happen to you, darling. Nothing. I won't let it."

"I'll be all right," Rock said. "I'll manage, sweetheart."

The sheriff took her arm and led her away, and Meg was almost grateful for his support. Her legs were wobbly. She felt completely drained of strength. She walked back to the office and through it in a complete fog. Until she was out in the rain again and could feel the cold drive of it in her face, she wasn't able to think. Then, as she started home a flash thought struck her. What if the gun wasn't enough to help Rock get away? What if he had to fight his way out? What if he had to kill Henry Sale, or if the sheriff killed him?

She turned and looked back toward the jail, listening, almost sure that in another instant she would hear the sound of gunfire.

8

Rock Wesley examined the gun Meg had brought him, then tucked it under his belt. He felt a new surge of hope—a tingling excitement gripped him. The Meg he had seen a moment ago was hardly the same girl who had warned him away from trouble. This was a woman plunging headlong into desperate trouble to save a man she hardly knew. He tried to figure it, and it made just one kind of sense. He remembered his first conversations with her, his appreciation of her. She could have done this for one reason only—in trouble or not, they belonged together . . . he and Meg McAlpin.

Rock took a brief turn around his cell. He came back to the barred door and stood listening, but could hear nothing. After a moment he called the sheriff, and when there was no immediate answer, raised his voice to a shouting pitch. "Sale! Sale, I want to see you. Sale, come back here!"

After a minute of this the sheriff appeared at the jail doorway.

"What do you want?"

"I want to talk to you. Come here. I want to explain about Meg and the McAlpins. I want to make a deal."

That seemed to be the bait to use. The sheriff

came toward him, came to the door, and stopped. "What about you and the McAlpins?"

"We'll get to that later," Rock said. "First, I want to show you this."

He drew the gun Meg had brought him.

Henry Sale caught his breath. He took one backward step, lifting his hands shoulder high. He shook his head numbly from side to side. "No, Lafferty! No!"

"Unlock the door, Sale. Leave the key in the lock. Then step back."

Sale reached for his keys. He fumbled with them, found the key to the cell door and unlocked it. He backed away as Rock stepped into the corridor.

Rock strode forward, took Sale's sidegun, dropped it in his pocket, then gave the sheriff a shove toward the open cell. "Get in there," he ordered.

The sheriff backed into the cell. Rock closed and locked the door, then took the keys.

"We'll talk, now, sheriff," he said gruffly. "I want you to listen to what I've got to say."

"You can't leave me in here," Sale mumbled. "You can't—"

"Listen to me," Rock said. "You won't be here long. Someone will find you. When that happens you'll have some explaining to do, but leave the McAlpins out if it, understand? Don't even say that Meg McAlpin came here. You can say this gun was in my boot, that you didn't find it when you searched me last night. If you don't think that sounds convincing, think of something else. But if you make trouble for the McAlpins, I'll come back and kill you some day."

Rock turned and hurried to the office. He started toward the street door, but stopped halfway. The heavy door was opening. Someone was coming in. He raised his gun and stood waiting.

The door swung wide. Tom Garmish stepped inside. He saw Rock and the gun, and his body went rigid. Then his hands lifted slowly until they were above his head, and he gasped, "You—Wesley!"

"You used the right name, anyhow," Rock said. "Peel off your slicker."

Garmish unbuttoned his slicker, took it off, and held it out to Rock. He was careful to keep his hand clear from his gun.

Rock took the slicker with his left hand; his right, with the gun, slashed out. The heavy barrel caught Garmish under the chin; his knees folded and he dropped to the floor.

Rock took Garmish's gun, tucked it in his belt, then put on the slicker and Garmish's hat. The last was a little tight, but better than no hat at all. Stepping to the doorway, he glanced up and down the street. The horse Garmish had ridden to town was tied directly in front of the sheriff's office. It had a sturdy, rugged look.

Rock crossed the walk, unlooped the reins, and climbed to the saddle. He turned down the street and, at the corner, swung east. It still was raining quite hard. The streets were empty. He cut through the town toward the rolling hills beyond. A quarter of a mile from the last house, he looked back. Someone was hurrying after him at a driving gallop. He reached under his slicker for his gun, but didn't draw it. Instead he waited.

Meg McAlpin galloped up. "No trouble?"

He shook his head. "None to speak of, Meg. How can I ever thank you for what you did?"

"By forgetting the mares you lost, and heading for Sawtelle," Meg said promptly.

"And what of the men who were killed?"

"Nothing you can do will change that, Rock. You can't give them life again."

Rock took a deep breath. He stared soberly at the girl. "We're going to fight again, aren't we?"

"If you mean what I think, we are."

"I can't leave for Sawtelle. Not yet, Meg."

She straightened angrily. "Why not? What can you gain if you stay here? They'll gun you down—you'll die under an outlaw's name."

"It might not work out that way. What about Chenoweth?"

"He's our problem, Rock. Some day, someone will challenge him. Some day the people here will band together and stand against him. There's a right time for everything."

Rock said quietly, "Now's the right time for me to stand up to Chenoweth. Not when he's got me on the run—like he has you and a lot of other people here."

Anger struck across her face. She seemed close to tears. "You're stubborn and pig-headed and blind! Stick around. Get yourself killed. See if I care!"

She leaned forward, jabbing her heels at the flanks of her horse and loosening the reins. The horse leapt past Rock, broke into a gallop, then angled toward the road that would take her home. She looked back, once, but didn't slow down.

Rock followed her, more slowly, but at a point several miles from the town left the road and took shelter from the rain in a stand of timber along one of the creeks in the valley. He dismounted, tied his horse, hunkered down and lit his pipe. He doubted there would be any great effort at immediate pursuit; the rain would make tracking him difficult. Besides, Chenoweth would figure he was on his way out of the valley, which was all the other really wanted.

The day wore slowly on. By midafternoon the rain stopped, but the skies stayed gray and cold. Two riders Rock didn't recognize passed along the road, heading toward town. Later on, another man, alone, rode that way.

Rock waited miserably for darkness to come. He was soaked, chilled to the bone, and there were too many sore muscles in his body to be counted. As the shadows began to thicken he paced back and forth under the trees, trying to work out the stiffness which threatened to grip him. With nightfall he climbed into the saddle and headed back toward Modoc.

He left the road near town, slanted off into a side alley and pulled up, finally, behind Roy Seigel's office. He left his horse ground-hitched, stepped up to the door and knocked.

Seigel threw his door wide. "Damn you, Rock! I thought you'd be miles away from here by now—come on in, dammit, man!"

Rock stepped into the narrow back room, pulled the door shut behind him. He glanced toward the stove. Something cooking there smelled good.

Seigel said, "My cooking isn't as good as my liquor, but what I've got, we'll share. Pull a chair up to the table. Anyone know you're here?"

"Don't think so. Meg McAlpin might guess."

"Who were the two men who helped you out of jail?"

"Two men?"

"That's the sheriff's story. He says two men jumped him early this morning, put their guns on him, locked him up and set you free. He says he didn't know them. It's his guess and the guess of a good many others that the men were outlaw friends of yours—your real name being Ringo Lafferty."

"And what does Garmish say?"

"He says that you and the two others were searching the sheriff's desk when he came in. The two strangers gun-covered him. Under their guns, you pistol-whipped him and knocked him out."

Rock nodded, amused and pleased at the story the sheriff had invented. He sat down at the table, rubbing his hands and wrists. Seigel put a steaming plate of soup in front of him, poured coffee, and set out the bread.

"Didn't guess you'd manage to break jail," Seigel said. "Maybe the wire I sent wasn't necessary."

"What wire?"

"A wire to the sheriff in Sawtelle, explaining you had been arrested and identified as Ringo Lafferty, and asking his suggestions."

"Any answer?"

"This came about an hour ago. The station master brought it over."

Seigel handed him a slip of paper. On it was scrawled, *"My representative on way to Modoc. Ken Wallace, Sheriff, Sawtelle."*

Rock was frowning as he passed the message back to the attorney. "I don't know whom Ken could mean," he said slowly. "He doesn't have a regular deputy."

"Then who would he be most likely to send?"

"That's hard to tell."

"I suppose the man will report to me. It'll take him maybe three days to get here. A lot can happen in three days. You haven't told me yet why you're still here."

"You thought I'd be riding away?"

"It would be the sensible thing to do."

"Do you think Chenoweth will figure that way, too?"

"Don't see why he shouldn't."

"Then that's why I'm here. If Chenoweth figures I'm gone, it gives me an edge on him."

"But how much of an edge, Rock?"

"Maybe all I'll need. Who knows? I understand you've handled some land deals here. Got a map of the Modoc Valley? I want to study the range Chenoweth controls."

"You're after the mares you lost?"

"That's part of it," Rock admitted.

"If Chenoweth's holding them, they'll be guarded. Even if he figures you've left the country, he'll have his men on the lookout for you."

"Maybe. But get the map and let's have a look at it."

Seigel was gone only a few minutes. When he returned he had a rolled map under his arm. They spread it out on the table, and with his finger, Seigel traced the outline of Chenoweth's Arrowhead range. It took in a vast amount of territory and was watered by a dozen small creeks.

"It would take a man a month to search the Arrowhead thoroughly," the attorney said.

"But I have to search only until I find the mares," Rock said. "And I might be lucky. I might hit the right meadow the first week."

"You've got to keep under cover, too. How'll you manage that?"

Rock was busy making a small, crude tracing of the map. He didn't answer, but at the sound of a sudden hammering on the front door, he straightened.

"Could be anyone," Seigel said as he turned toward the front room. "Sit tight."

Rock heard him answer the door, and heard a man saying, "Chenoweth wants to see you right away, Seigel—up at the saloon."

"Tell him I'll be there as soon as I can make it," Seigel replied.

He closed and locked the door and returned to the back room. "Orders from the king," he said in a wry, bitter voice. "When Chenoweth speaks, everyone is supposed to jump. It's easier than bucking him."

"What'll he want?"

"Who knows?"

Rock folded the drawing he had made and put it in his pocket. He said, "Roy, I'll need some grub to take with me."

"Help yourself to what I've got. I'll lay in new supplies tomorrow, and a few extra things you can pick up any night you want to risk a trip to town."

Rock made a selection of enough staple foods to last him several days. These he sacked and carried out to his horse. Seigel went with him.

"Careful, Rock," the attorney advised. "You won't find any friends in the country you're riding into. The valley is even more scared of Chenoweth than the town."

"Thanks for all you've done, Roy."

Rock swung into saddle and picked his way through the houses clustered back of the Main Street. Beyond the outskirts of the town he circled to the north and west, crossed the Modoc River, and cut into the Arrowhead range. Somewhere up here, Chenoweth was holding his mares. What he would do if he found them, he didn't know. The first step was to find them.

9

Arne Chenoweth paced back and forth across the floor of the sheriff's office, pausing now and then to fire a question at Henry Sale or at Tom Garmish. Bealer Harrison stood at the door, keeping a casual watch on the street. Since Ollie Reed's death, Harrison had stepped into his place as foreman of the Arrowhead outfit. He was a big man, though gaunt, nearing fifty.

Henry Sale sat at his desk. Garmish stood behind him and to one side. Chenoweth stopped his pacing to stare at them.

"Damn it, I don't believe it," he grated. "You tell me two men came here to bust Wesley out of jail. I'm asking you once more, what two men?"

"How the hell do I know?" Garmish snapped. "Anyway, I came in wearing a slicker. How can a man wearing a buttoned-up slicker make a play for his gun?"

Chenoweth made an angry motion with his arm. "Shut up, Garmish. I want to hear what Sale's got to say."

"I've said all I've got to say," the sheriff rumbled. "Do you think I'm happy about what happened?"

"No. I think you're lying, that's all. I don't believe there were any two men. Or if there were, I don't believe they were strangers. Where the hell would two strangers come from to help Wesley? We killed the two men he had with him. The rest of his crew are miles from here. Maybe two men from town or from somewhere else around here helped him. If that's it, I want to know who they were."

"And I said I didn't know them," Sale answered. "They weren't from around here."

"Like hell they weren't. Was Seigel one?"

"No. He wouldn't have the guts for it."

"Jim Fleming?"

"Hell no. Fleming's just a kid. Besides, he's not in town. I tell you, the men were strangers."

"You're lying!"

The sheriff's face turned a brick red. He was breathing heavily. He came half to his feet, but after this momentary show of resentment, sank back in his chair again, his hands tightly gripped together. When he spoke he sounded tired. "I'm not lying, Arne. I didn't know the two men."

Chenoweth gave Garmish a scorching glance, then swung around and crossed to the window. He stood there, staring into the street, but unconscious of anything he saw. He knew that the story Garmish and Henry Sale had told him wasn't true. They were lying to cover up what actually had happened. They were lying to excuse themselves for Wesley's escape. They were also covering up for someone in town.

Garmish broke the silence. "Arne?"

"What is it?" Chenoweth asked without looking around.

"We're not getting anywhere like this. I want to go after him."

"After who?"

"Wesley."

Chenoweth jerked to face him. "You want to go after Wesley? What about the two men who helped him escape?"

"I'll take care of them at the same time."

Chenoweth's eyes narrowed. He checked the thoughts running through his mind. While they were together, he couldn't break down the story Sale and Garmish had obviously agreed on. Alone, either man might crack. Chenoweth was sure now that Garmish, at least, had seen no strangers; he would not be eager to track three armed men in this storm. Sale probably had invented the strangers to explain his having been locked in his own jail—and Garmish had adopted the story. What had happened was that Wesley, in some way or other, had gotten his hands on a gun, locked the sheriff up, and in escaping, had run into Garmish.

"Well, how about it?" Garmish asked.

Chenoweth shrugged. Now he was staring at the sheriff. He said, "Go ahead, Tom. If you can follow a trail through this rain, follow it."

"Don't worry," Garmish said gruffly. "I'll find him. I'll bring in his ears."

"And what about the other two men?" Chenoweth asked, a touch of sarcasm in his voice.

"They're good as dead right now," Garmish said, heading for the door.

Chenoweth stood staring at the sheriff. He waited until Garmish was gone, then spoke quietly. "There were no two strangers, Henry. In some way or other, Wesley got a gun, locked you up, then covered Garmish when he came in from the street. Tell me this—did you give him the gun?"

He had chosen the right attack this time. Sale had not expected the last question. Chenoweth could tell that by the frightened look that jumped into the sheriff's eyes, and by the way Sale's face tightened.

"Come on, Henry," he insisted. "Speak up. Tell me what happened. The truth, this time."

"I—told you the truth."

Chenoweth glanced over his shoulder toward the door. "Anyone coming this way, Bealer?"

"Nope. No one at all."

Chenoweth took off his coat, rolled up his sleeves. He had thick, hard forearms, big fists. He held them up and his eyes brightened. He said, "Henry, you've one more chance to tell the truth. If I don't get the story, and get it straight, I'll beat it out of you. Start talking."

Henry Sale was perspiring. Suddenly he said, "It was Meg McAlpin, Arne. I didn't know she had a gun—she said she'd get a gun if I didn't let her see him. I knew how you felt about her—and I didn't know there was anything between them. I didn't—"

"Meg McAlpin," Chenoweth repeated. "Meg McAlpin. I don't believe it!"

He felt rocked, confused. In spite of the way she constantly had put him off and avoided him, he had always promised himself that some day he would marry Meg McAlpin. He had been confident of his ability to wear down her defenses. He hadn't rushed things with her, afraid that to be too aggressive would be wrong.

Now he thought perhaps he should have rushed things a little. Maybe he should have just taken her one night in town. He knew she hadn't been entirely averse to him—and some women needed a whip now and then.

But these were empty thoughts. He knew he could never have taken force to Meg McAlpin.

Chenoweth straightened. "So you let a woman in to see him. Why the hell didn't you search her first?"

"I told you—she made me believe she didn't have a gun. That she was going to get one—" Sale blushed suddenly, furiously, all over his fat, perspiring face. God, what an act she'd put on!

Chenoweth turned and walked to the window and stood looking into the street, without seeing it. He told himself that it really didn't make so much difference that Wesley had escaped. The man had no place to turn for help, and eventually, today, tomorrow, or next week, Tom Garmish would pick up his trail, follow him, and even the score between them. Tom had no qualms about shooting a man in the back.

But that was one thing. What he had learned about Meg was another. He almost wished he hadn't pressed so hard to get at the truth, but there it was, ugly to look at. He was beginning to get angry, now. He had offered Meg a position finer than that held by any other woman in the valley. She could have been mistress of the Arrowhead. Instead, she had given herself to a stranger.

He could see it in no other way. Unless a woman loved a man, she wouldn't risk what Meg had risked for Rock Wesley. It had to be like that, but damn it, he didn't have to take it lying down. And he didn't have to be a gentleman any longer, so far as Meg was concerned. Next time he saw her . . .

A sudden fear struck him—Meg might have fled with Wesley. He glanced at Bealer Harrison and said, "Bealer, Meg stayed in town last night with her sister. See if she's still there. If she's not, find out where she went and when she left. And don't say a damned word to anyone about what you heard in here."

"Sure, Arne." Bealer Harrison nodded.

Chenoweth then walked to the door. From there, he looked back at Henry Sale.

"We'll let the story about the two strangers stand, as you told it," he said gruffly. "But I'll have a few things to say to you privately, later on, Henry. One more mistake and you're finished in Modoc. Understand?"

The sheriff made a weak affirmative motion.

Chenoweth walked through the slackening rain to the Golden Horseshoe saloon. By now, if Wesley and Meg McAlpin were heading out of the valley, they had several hours' start, and there wasn't anything he could do about that. He had a drink, and then another. Bealer Harrison came in to report that according to her sister, Meg had headed for home that morning.

"Find out if she went there," he ordered.

It was late evening before Harrison got back to Modoc. By that time, Chenoweth had had so much to drink he was slightly groggy.

"She's at the ranch," Harrison told him.

"And Wesley?"

"I don't think he's there. I slipped up on the house in the dark and took a look through the windows. The girl was sewing, the old man reading. No sign of anyone else around."

Chenoweth felt a sudden lift in spirits. He didn't know why Meg hadn't fled with Wesley, but he was deeply thankful that she had not. It meant he could see her again, and without too much trouble. He slammed his fist into the palm of his hand and came to his feet, nodding. He had been careful never to run into an open conflict with Ed McAlpin, chiefly on account of Meg, but the necessity for that was over.

"Get the men together," he ordered. "We're heading home."

He returned his bottle to the bar, went outside. The moist smell of the rain still was in the air, but the sky was clearing and it was chilly. He turned up the collar of his coat, leaned back against the saloon wall, and projected his thoughts into the future. The Temple Hills outlaws were going to be heard from again. They would smash the McAlpin ranch, this time, burn it to the ground, and get away with most of McAlpin's cattle.

He started laughing when he thought of the Temple Hills outlaws. McAlpin would take what happened, just as others had taken it. He could kick up a fuss and get himself killed, or he would fade out of the picture. As for Meg, he would decide later how she was to be treated. There was no hurry. To set up the raid, properly, would take two or three days.

Rock Wesley had searched along the course of three streams watering the Arrowhead range without finding a trace of the missing mares. He next made a skirting survey of the valley meadows to the north, but without success. The conviction was growing in his mind that the mares were being held somewhere quite close to the main ranch house. That would be the next area he would explore, but before he did he needed a fresh batch of supplies. He was almost out of food.

He checked his approximate location on the map he had made in Seigel's office. By the map, he was about five miles north of the Arrowhead headquarters and eight miles west of the Modoc River. He could follow the stream below him to the river and turn down the river to town. If he started that way now, he could reach town by early evening, and most of the way would have the shelter of screening trees.

Or he could try something else. He could ride east, cross the river, and continue due east to the McAlpin ranch. He could make it there by dusk, and on the way have a look at some of the Arrowhead land east of the river.

He put away his map, dropped down the hillside to the stream, and turned east. He was still debating which of the two courses he would follow when he came to the Modoc River, but this argument with himself actually was no more than a foolish mental exercise. In the back of his mind he knew that when he reached the Modoc River he would cross it and ride on east to the McAlpin ranch. He had made that decision the day before. He wanted to see Meg again. He wanted another chance to talk to her. The brief conversation they had had in the rain on the outskirts of town after she had helped him escape from jail had been too short, too inconclusive. It hadn't even touched on things between them that needed to be said.

He crossed the Modoc River and rode on east. He found few cattle over here. West of the river there had been small herds of cattle in almost every valley meadow he had seen, and the Arrowhead was a big ranch. At a guess, Chenoweth might be able to tally ten thousand head on the land he owned. Or even more. It was no wonder that he was an important man in this part of the country.

It still was light when Rock Wesley pulled up in the yard of the McAlpin ranch house. Meg came out to the porch. She was wearing boots, Levi's, and a blue shirt, and if she was surprised or pleased to see him, she didn't show it.

She said, "Hello, Rock," and took a quick look to the west.

"Don't think anyone's following me," Rock said. "Was I wrong to come here?"

She shook her head. "No. Put your horse in the barn and come inside. I'll get you some supper."

He felt a little uncomfortable as he rode to the barn, dismounted and tended to his horse. He reminded himself that he shouldn't have expected a warmer welcome. Anyone who sheltered him was risking the anger of Arne Chenoweth, and to no advantage to themselves.

"Might as well unsaddle your horse and stay

the night," Ed McAlpin called from the barn doorway.

Rock looked around, then waved his hand in greeting, but made a negative motion with his head. "I'll be riding on in a few hours."

"No sense in it," McAlpin said. "Glad you stopped by. Find your mares?"

"No."

"The Arrowhead's a big ranch. It would take a man a month to cover it all."

"Then I'll take a month," Rock said.

He left his horse saddled, joined McAlpin in the doorway, and they turned toward the house.

"Don't reckon you've been seen," McAlpin mentioned. "Jim Fleming dropped by last night. He tells me the general opinion in town is that you got out of the Modoc Valley fast as you could ride."

"What about the jail break?"

"Two of your friends showed up, gun-covered the sheriff and put him in the cell in your place. When Garmish came in they disarmed him and knocked him over the head. Garmish and the sheriff stuck together on that story."

Rock smiled. "You know the truth."

"Yes. Meg told me what she did. She ought to be whipped for the risk she took, but I'm kind of proud of her."

"I don't blame you for that," Rock said.

They had stopped near the front steps. McAlpin

was scowling. He scuffed his boots in the dirt. He said, "Rock, I suppose I ought to tell you this. Meg has a high sense of what is right and what is wrong. Everything's black or white. There's not much middle ground to her way of thinking, but circumstances have forced her to balance on a middle ground. It's like this. Arne Chenoweth is a powerful man, and this ranch of mine is right under his guns. He isn't married, and for more than a year now he's been showing an interest in Meg. Normally, Meg is as quick as a flash with a yes or no, but in this instance, she's been stalling, and it hasn't been an easy thing to do."

"She's been stalling to keep Chenoweth from moving in on you."

"That's it. I haven't asked her to. In fact, I've told her a dozen times to give Chenoweth a definite no, but she won't talk to me about him. Things can't go on this way, of course. Sooner or later Chenoweth's going to demand an answer. Did you ever try running a ranch while you were looking down into the barrel of a gun? It isn't easy."

"But doesn't Meg see what lies ahead?"

"Maybe she won't let herself."

"You don't think she'd marry him?"

"No. She'd never go that far. Besides, she knows I wouldn't stand for it."

They went inside, where Rock sat down to the best meal he had had in days. Afterwards, he spread out on the table the map he had drawn, and showed McAlpin and Meg the territory he had covered in his search. "Next, I'll look here," he told them, and with his finger he circled the location of the Arrowhead main buildings.

"A risky business," McAlpin said, frowning. "But if Chenoweth has your mares, he's probably holding them close to home."

"I came here because I was running short of food," Rock said.

"We can let you have what you need," McAlpin said. "Meg, why don't you—"

He broke off and raised his head in the attitude of someone listening. Rock, also, had tensed, aware of the sound of drumming hoofbeats.

"Someone coming," Meg said.

She hurried to the window. Rock joined her there. The night shadows were thickening but there still was light in the sky—enough to show them the four riders heading toward the house.

McAlpin said uneasily, "Don't know who it could be. We don't often have folks drop by here at night."

"Maybe I'd better get out of sight," Rock suggested.

"Take him to your room, Meg," McAlpin said.

Meg took him there. "They may be some men from town," she said. "People we know. In any case, you'll be safe enough in here."

She sounded as worried as her father.

"I shouldn't have come here," Rock said. "But I wanted to see you again. I wanted to thank you again for helping me out of jail. I'm glad, for your sake, that the truth of what happened isn't known."

"But I think it is known—to Arne Chenoweth," Meg said. "I was in town yesterday and saw him for a minute on the street. He didn't act like he usually does when he meets me. He was different. Rock, I'm a little frightened."

They were standing close together, just inside the door to her room. Rock took her hand. He said, "Don't be, Meg. Things will work out."

She shook her head. "I wish I was sure of that. Wait here—I'll leave the door open a crack so you can hear what's said."

10

The four riders pulled up in the yard of the McAlpin ranch. They were part of a larger group which had headed this way from the Arrowhead, shortly after noon. The others who had come with them had angled on down the valley to round up McAlpin's cattle, and start them running into the hills. These four had a special assignment. Each knew the part he had to play in the task ahead.

Max Durbin glanced at his companions, singling out Tad Ellander. He said, "Tad, make your play as soon as Royce has taken care of the girl and brought her outside. I'll cover for you. Then we'll start the fire."

"What if McAlpin isn't wearing his gun?" Ellander asked.

"That should make your work twice as easy."

"The girl may kick up a ruckus," Royce said.

"You're bigger than she is, ain't you?" Durbin said. "Let's go."

They dismounted and handed the reins of their horses to the fourth man, who would hold them while they were inside. And as they started toward the house the door opened and McAlpin appeared in the entrance.

"We're from the Arrowhead," Durbin called. "Got a message for you from Arne Chenoweth."

"Come on in," McAlpin said.

He had little choice in the matter, and realized it. The three men climbing the porch steps seemed to take it for granted that they would be invited inside. He stepped back from the door, and as the men came in he recognized Durbin and Ellander. Royce he had seen before but didn't know by name.

Meg had come back from her room and was facing the three men who had just come in. McAlpin noticed how tense she looked. He said, "Meg, see if there's any coffee left. I think you know Max Durbin and Tad Ellander, and—"

"I'm Fred Royce," the third man said.

Meg went to the stove. From a crock on a stand near it, she added water to the coffee.

"What's on Arne's mind?" McAlpin asked.

"He's got something for your daughter," Durbin said. "He wants her to come to the Arrowhead tonight."

Meg stiffened. She whirled to face Max Durbin. "If Arne Chenoweth wants to see me, let him come here."

"He can't do that, ma'am," Durbin said. "All right, Royce."

Royce started toward her, a grin showing on his face. He said, "Come on, girl. We're gonna have a nice, long ride together."

"We're going to do no such thing," Meg snapped.

Royce lunged suddenly forward. He caught her in his arms, but with a violent twist of her body, Meg broke free. She grabbed the coffee pot from the stove and swung it at Royce. It struck his shoulder as he tried to duck. The hot liquid spilled over him and brought a howl of protest from his lips.

In the next room, Rock Wesley held himself in check. Through the partly open door, he saw Royce grab at Meg, saw Meg break free and slam him with the coffeepot. Across the room, Durbin had drawn his gun, stepped close to McAlpin, and shoved it against his side. "Keep out of this, McAlpin," he had warned. "She's not gonna be hurt. She's just going with us for a little ride."

Rock was leaning forward, his gun leveled. He saw Meg struggling with Royce as the latter dragged her toward the door and it flashed across his mind that if he didn't break into the room until Meg was outside, she at least would be safe from the danger of a stray bullet. The thought helped to steady him. His main worry was McAlpin—once these men got Meg outside, they would have to kill the rancher. They couldn't risk what McAlpin would tell if he got to town. He hadn't been killed yet because of Meg. Chenoweth probably wanted to bargain with her . . . a fury such as he had never known rose in Rock Wesley, but curiously it, too, helped to hold him back.

Royce now had Meg at the door, and a moment later succeeded in pulling her outside.

Durbin spoke again. "Tad," he said, "Close the front door."

This brought the other man into Rock's range of vision. He watched Tad Ellander cross the room and shut the door.

McAlpin's face was beady with perspiration. His eyes had a wide, staring look. He probably had guessed what lay ahead. He probably knew how thin his chances were. He spoke slowly, as though choosing his words with care in the hope that they would make an impression on the men still in the room with him.

"Chenoweth's gone too far, this time. Too many people in the valley think highly of Meg to let him get away with it. Everyone who had a part in this will be hunted down."

Durbin stepped away from him. He still held his gun leveled at McAlpin. There was an ugly, twisted look on his face. It had been planned that Ellander would handle this part of the job, but his gun already covered the man who was to be killed.

"McAlpin," he rasped, "Your gun's hangin' over the fireplace. I'll give you a chance to get it."

McAlpin didn't say a word. He turned and started across the room but before he had taken two steps, Durbin's gun arm reached out and steadied, and Rock knew that McAlpin wasn't to be given even the chance he had been promised.

Rock's gun was already aimed. He pressed the trigger, and saw Durbin stiffen, turn half around, then plunge to the floor.

A sharp, startled cry broke from Tad Ellander's lips. The man whirled toward the partially open bedroom door, whipping up his gun. Rock's bullet took him full in the chest.

Ellander took a step forward. He dropped his gun, then followed it to the floor.

Rock moved on into the room. McAlpin's face was still shiny with perspiration. The room seemed terribly still now, and into its silence McAlpin spoke, his words coming out in a husky whisper. "They meant to kill me. They wouldn't have given me a chance. Would Arne Chenoweth have planned a thing like this?"

"You'll have to answer that question yourself," Rock said. "Wait here—they expected some gunshots, but we may have given them too many. I'll see about Meg."

He moved quickly to the rear of the house, slid open a window and slipped outside. The front yard was quiet now, except for the restive movement of horses. Then, as he rounded the house, Rock heard a curse and a scream.

In the faint light remaining, he saw that Meg was still struggling—or was struggling again—with Fred Royce. Another man, mounted and holding the reins of the other three horses, was eyeing the house uneasily.

Rock fired without aiming, sending a bullet in the general direction of the mounted man, but with his eyes on Royce. He had killed before in self-defense—now for the first time in his life he felt a deliberate, hot urge to take a life. He didn't give a damn about the man on the horse—he wanted to kill Royce.

At the sound of his shot, Royce dropped the girl, threw one hurried look over his shoulder, then ran for his horse.

Rock fired deliberately—but was forced to shift his aim at the last instant as Meg rose from the ground, almost in his line of fire, and came running toward him. He saw Royce go down, heard the receding beat of hoofs as the mounted man made his getaway.

Then Meg was in his arms, her clothes torn, her hair disheveled, gasping, "What about dad— those shots in the house—"

"He's all right," he told her. "He should be out in a minute—" He had one arm around Meg, but he wasn't thinking of her at this moment.

When McAlpin came out, presently, he was still holding her so, and was still watching the dark mass on the ground that was Fred Royce. He didn't know how badly Royce had been hit.

McAlpin took Meg from him, and without looking at either of them, Rock stalked to where

Royce was lying, and knelt down briefly. Royce had been hit through the shoulder. He was bleeding heavily, and was unconscious. Rock wanted to put another bullet through him—then, abruptly, his anger left him. He was suddenly tired, and stood up and turned back to where Meg and her father were standing.

McAlpin still seemed dazed at what had happened. "I just can't believe it," he said in a half whisper. "It's like a nightmare. If you hadn't been here, Wesley—"

"That was something they didn't figure on," Rock said. "When they rode here they thought they'd find only you and Meg."

The older man nodded gravely. "This finishes Chenoweth. When they hear of this in Modoc—"

"How will you tell it?"

"Just as it happened."

"And Chenoweth will deny every word you say. He may even deny anyone was killed if he can get the bodies away from here before you get back with the sheriff. Or he can say he had fired the four men who came here and they were acting on their own."

"Then what can I do?"

"Get to town—at least you can be safe there. For what it's worth, send the sheriff back here in a hurry, with as many men you can trust as you can find."

"I'll have to say you were here."

"Sheriff's bound to find that out, sooner or later."

"And you're still labeled an outlaw. That gives Chenoweth another out. He can say the men were after you."

"Which doesn't help matters any."

McAlpin shrugged wearily. "I'll get my hat and coat, and a blouse and jacket for you, Meg. Wait out here. I don't want you to go inside."

He started for the door, hurrying. Meg looked at Rock. She said, "They're dead, aren't they—the two men inside?"

He nodded, without speaking.

After a while she said, "Whatever I did for you in town—you've paid it back tonight. You were right about Chenoweth—and everything. What are you going to do now?"

He said gruffly, "Round up some horses to take you and your father to town. After that, we'll see."

They left a few minutes later, taking the road to Modoc. It was Meg who looked back and who first saw the red glow in the sky behind them. She reined up, calling, "Father! Rock!"

They stopped, looked around, and McAlpin swore softly under his breath.

Rock said nothing. He knew, just as they did, what it was that had cast the red glow into the sky. Someone had fired McAlpin's ranch house and barn.

McAlpin leaned forward in his saddle, staring

at the red glow. He pushed back his hat, and glanced at Rock. "I'm getting the full picture now," he said slowly. "This same thing happened once before, and not far from here, to a man named Bledsoe. His ranch was burned down and the same night his cattle were driven off—by the Temple Hills outlaws—another name for Chenoweth's riders."

"And Bledsoe?" Rock asked.

"He rode into the hills with the sheriff's posse, trailing his lost cattle. The trail faded out on the claybanks. He came back to town and got into a row in a poker game and got shot by an Arrowhead rider. The bank foreclosed on his property and still owns it. The bank is owned by Chenoweth."

"So what are you going to do, Ed? Ride with the sheriff's posse on a useless chase into the hills, return to town, and then get into a row with an Arrowhead rider and get shot?"

"No, by God!"

"It can happen. If you go around making charges that Chenoweth's men burned your place down."

"Then what do I do—take this lying down?"

"No. You wait."

"Wait for what?"

"If I can find where Chenoweth is hiding my mares, we can get a crowd together and nail him red-handed."

The red glow in the sky was brighter. Rock glanced at Meg. She looked spent, ready to drop. McAlpin seemed suddenly much older. His shoulders sagged.

"I'm in debt to the bank, just like most other ranchers," he said slowly. "With the loss of my cattle I won't be able to meet the interest payments on my loans. And where could I borrow money to rebuild my house and barn? Chenoweth's got me over a barrel."

"From what you've told me, he's got the whole valley over a barrel," Rock said. "But if I can prove he's got my mares, he's vulnerable. Do this—make your report to the sheriff. Let Chenoweth lie out of it. Then sit and wait. Don't get sucked into a fight, Ed. Keep out of Chenoweth's way and avoid his men like poison. Give me a chance to find my mares. Give me a chance to pin something on him he can't lie out of."

"I suppose you know Chenoweth will have every man he has out searching for you the minute he realizes you still are in this part of the country. If he's got your horses, he'll guard them better."

"Maybe."

"What chance does that give you?"

"Who knows, Ed? You play the cards the way they're dealt. We don't hold much of a hand right now. Maybe they will freeze us out before we can make a call—or maybe on the next deal we'll come up with three aces. Let's see what happens."

They rode on. Behind them, the red glow in the sky gradually faded. Finally, it could be seen no more.

11

Roy Seigel carried the coffeepot from the stove to the table. He poured coffee for himself and the McAlpins, tried to think of something cheerful to say, but couldn't. He could find no way to help them. Two days before when McAlpin and his daughter had ridden into town with their story of the raid on their ranch, Chenoweth had bluntly denied that any of his men could have been involved.

He had accompanied the posse that rode back. They had found the ranch and barn, burned to the ground, but no sign of bodies, and Chenoweth, with the sheriff in agreement, placed the blame for the raid on the Temple Hills outlaws. His men, now, theoretically, were making a grim effort to ride the outlaws down, and to clear them out of the hills. Actually, they were conducting a careful search for Rock Wesley, and Seigel was afraid they would find him.

"I'm coming to the point of hating myself," McAlpin muttered. "I didn't call Chenoweth when he lied. I backed down when he offered to let me go along with his men on a chase after the outlaws. And here in town I've been keeping out of sight like a man who was afraid of his own shadow."

"What else could you do?" Seigel asked. "You can't fight Chenoweth alone."

"Rock Wesley's doing just that."

"And right now, in all probability, he's hiding, just as you are. There's no shame in hiding until you're ready to make your play, Ed. It's the man who quits who is a coward."

"Haven't I quit?"

"I wouldn't say so."

"It amounts to the same thing."

Meg looked at Seigel. "Rock's all right, isn't he? As long as we don't hear anything, doesn't it mean that he's safe?"

"Probably."

Meg bit her lips. Her hands were tightly laced together in her lap. She had a mental picture of Rock, cornered somewhere in the hills by Chenoweth's men. She could see them closing in on him. She could imagine the sound of the gunfire. A shudder ran over her body. "I shouldn't have let him ride back there again," she said under her breath. "I should have made him go away."

She glanced at her father, noticed the bleak and hopeless look on his face and wished, just as Roy Seigel had wished a few moments before, that she could think of something cheerful to say, but the right words wouldn't come to her. She sampled her coffee. Even the coffee didn't taste good.

It was early evening, and for that reason, the knock on the front door didn't startle them. People often dropped by to see the attorney in the evening. He got up and left the room to see who was at the door. When he returned a few moments later, three men were with him, strangers, and all three were men to attract attention. One was big, broad-shouldered, heavy, and had a square, stubborn-looking face. One was thin, lean, freckled, redheaded and young. The third was thin, stooped, old, wrinkled, and had the leathery brown skin and the features of an Indian.

Seigel was obviously excited as he introduced them. "Ed," he said, "Meg, these men are from Sawtelle. They came here in response to my telegram. This is Ken Wallace, the sheriff of Sawtelle, and Jeff Elliott and Indian Charlie, who work for Rock."

The sheriff was the big, square-shouldered man. Jeff Elliott was the young man with the red hair and freckles. Indian Charlie was the one who looked like an Indian. He had black, deep-set eyes and wore moccasins instead of boots.

"We made it here fast as we could after getting your telegram," Wallace said. "What kind of trouble has Rock got himself into?"

"You might as well sit down," Seigel said. "It's a long story."

They still were sitting at the table an hour later.

McAlpin, Meg, and Roy Seigel had told the men from Sawtelle all they knew. The character and possible plans of Arne Chenoweth had been discussed, and his power here in the Modoc valley had been analyzed. Seigel didn't make the situation look any more hopeful than it was. "You may be a sheriff," he said to Wallace, "but I doubt if Henry Sale will recognize that you have any authority around here. He's too completely under the domination of Arne Chenoweth."

"And I don't have any authority around here," Wallace admitted. "He could be courteous enough to give me authority, but there's no law says he has to. I reckon we'll get little help from Sale."

"We'll get little help from anyone," McAlpin said bleakly. "I could name a dozen men who know Chenoweth is as bad as we've painted him, but not one is ready to do anything about it."

"Jim Fleming might throw in with us," Seigel said.

"Maybe Jim would, but who else?"

"Try a few others," Elliott suggested. "You might be surprised."

"But what can we offer them? What kind of plan do we have?"

"If Rock finds his mares on Arrowhead land, we'll have something to go on."

Jeff Elliott said, "If we want to find the Morgan mares, Charlie's the man to do it."

The Indian had said nothing. He said nothing now, but an appreciative gleam showed in his eyes.

"I think the first thing to do is to get Rock back in town," Wallace said. "We want to clear up this charge that he's Ringo Lafferty. Charlie, do you think you could find him for us?"

The Indian stood up. "I find him."

"McAlpin said he was going to search close to the Arrowhead ranch house," Wallace continued. "That's north and west of here, but that whole area will be alive with Chenoweth's riders. You'll have to be careful."

"I find him," the Indian said again.

"I have a map of the valley," Seigel said.

"Charlie make map in head as he hunt," the Indian said.

He turned and hurried from the room.

Meg was startled at the suddenness of the Indian's departure. Jeff Elliott noticed this, and said, "Never worry about Indian Charlie. He always moves like he's never been there. I don't know how old he is, but he can run all day and sleep so lightly it don't seem like sleep at all. He'll ride his horse to somewhere near the Chenoweth ranch house, hide it, then set out on foot. If Rock's anywhere nearby, Charlie will be on his trail by dawn."

"No man's that good," McAlpin said.

"You just don't know him," Wallace said.

"Charlie can follow a trail in water, seems like. I've seen him do it. Rock's father once saved his life. Charlie's still paying for it. Rock couldn't lose him if he wanted to, but I don't imagine he wants to."

"That high mesa country around Sawtelle must be nice country," Meg McAlpin said wistfully.

"It is." Wallace grinned at her. "And Rock's pretty well thought of, out that way. So were the men of his who were killed. I could have brought fifty riders with me if I'd known we might need 'em. I wish now I had."

Meg knew why she suddenly was feeling so much better. These three men from Sawtelle were responsible for it. They didn't seem overwhelmed by the problems they faced. They had heard the worst she and her father and Seigel could say of Arne Chenoweth without being unduly impressed. They gave her new hope.

"We'll wait until Rock gets here before we plan any further," Wallace said. "But in the meantime, I'll go up the street, see the sheriff and have a talk with him. Jeff, you might hit a few of the saloons and listen to what people are saying. Get us a double room at the hotel."

Jeff Elliott stood up. He was almost as tall as Rock. He had a friendly grin that reached his eyes and masked whatever he was thinking. He nodded.

"Sure enough, Ken."

"We'll see you folks later," Wallace said.

After the two had left the room, Seigel looked at the McAlpins. He rubbed his hands together. "This could be our break—what do you think?"

"They don't have any idea what they're going up against," McAlpin said. "They haven't lived with it like we have."

"Maybe they can see it better because they haven't lived with it," Meg said. "I liked them, Roy. Whatever they're in favor of doing, I'm in favor of doing."

"Then we'll just mark time for a while," Seigel said. "We'll see what tomorrow brings."

A stream of water twisting through the hills half-circled the Arrowhead main buildings. Its banks were heavily wooded. Rock Wesley had made a temporary camp within sight and almost within sound of the Arrowhead. By day he remained hidden, now and then dozing, but much of the time keeping a watch on the ranch house and on the arrival and departure of Chenoweth's riders. By night he ventured out in a persistent and narrowing search for his lost Morgan mares. He had covered most of the sheltered meadows to the north and west. Next, he would ride south.

This morning, as the sun came up, he watched

the activity in the ranch yard. After breakfast, Chenoweth came outside and, with six men, struck off on the road toward town. Eight men took off in a northerly direction and two rode south, these groups probably heading out on some operational detail. That their chief assignment was to try and pick up his trail was something he didn't know. Four men were left at the ranch, undoubtedly as guards.

As the morning wore on, things quieted down. Rock moved deeper into the trees along the creek and, in a tangle of shrubbery, stretched out on his blanket. A small breeze sang through the trees and the crackling of dead wood and the twittering of the birds was a normal background of familiar sounds. He dozed for a time, then awoke suddenly, unaware of what it was that had disturbed him, but strangely tense and uneasy. For a time he lay motionless, listening, straining his ears to catch any unfamiliar sound, but whatever it was that had reached through his unconsciousness to wake him wasn't repeated.

He got to his knees, his senses keening. After a moment, he stood up. His horse was tied at a spot even deeper in the trees. He headed that way, slowly, careful to make no sound. He came within sight of his horse. It was tied where he had left it, but wasn't grazing. It stood, facing almost toward him, its ears pricked forward.

A chill raced over his body. Someone else was here—hidden. Waiting. He stood motionless, his hand resting on his holstered gun.

"Rock Wesley," said a quiet voice to his left.

He swung toward the sound, whipping up his gun. But he didn't use it. The slight, stooped figure which moved into view was familiar. The hissing of his name was familiar.

"Charlie!" Rock whispered. "Where did you drop from?"

The Indian grinned. It wasn't often that any expression at all showed on his face, but on rare occasions his usual stoic look would break down. This was one of those times.

"We thought us needed," he answered.

"You and who else?"

"Wallace. Jeff."

"Not Ken Wallace. How did he get away?"

The Indian shrugged, as though that problem didn't concern him.

"Where are they? In Modoc?"

"Waiting for you. Go there tonight. I will find the mares."

Rock felt as though a great load had fallen from his shoulders. He knew his troubles weren't over, but they were suddenly simplified. If his mares were anywhere in this part of the country, no one could find them more quickly or surely than Indian Charlie. And in Modoc he had two men to stand with him who would be hard to equal, no matter what kind of fight they might run into. Ken Wallace was a rugged, two-fisted battler, and Jeff loved nothing better than a good brawl. He was no longer alone.

He walked up to Indian Charlie, squeezed the small shoulders and laughed in pure relief. Then he hunkered down on his heels near a thick tree trunk, Charlie near him. He filled and lit his pipe and took a deep drag on it.

"Who did you talk to in town?" he asked.

"Seigel, McAlpin, a woman named Meg," Charlie answered.

"Good. Then you got the story. You know what we're up against. The men from this ranch house near here are men to be avoided. To them, murder is nothing."

Indian Charlie shrugged.

"I have hunted to the north and west, without finding the mares," Rock continued. "Tonight I would have searched to the south. There are many small meadows and valleys among these hills. I feel that the mares are being held in such a place, not far from here. There are fifteen of them, Charlie."

"I find them," Charlie said.

"When you do, come to town and let us know where they are."

"Maybe I bring them to town."

"No, I want them left where you find them. I want to show people Chenoweth stole them."

"A bullet would be quicker end for man like him."

"It may come to that, too," Rock admitted. "But I will need to show the mares are here to justify the bullet. Just find them, and let us know where they are being held. That's all, Charlie."

"I find them." Charlie nodded. "You sleep now."

Rock left for Modoc shortly after dark. He made a wide circle around the Arrowhead headquarters, then took a course paralleling the road. It was well into the evening when he reached Roy Seigel's office.

Seigel grinned. "So they were right about Indian Charlie. I couldn't believe what they said about him. How did he find you?"

"I didn't ask him," Rock said. "Charlie wouldn't have made anything of it if I had. He was sent after me, he found me. I asked him to find the mares. I'll give you even money he's in here by tomorrow night to tell us where they are."

"A man like that is worth his weight in gold," Seigel said.

"More than that. Charlie's loyal, too. You couldn't buy his kind with all the money that's ever been minted. Where are Wallace and Jeff Elliott?"

"Wait here and I'll get them. Put out the lights. If anyone knocks on the door, don't answer it. I'd better get rid of your horse, too. I know an empty barn near here where I can stable it."

When Seigel returned with Ken Wallace and Jeff Elliott, the latter two were grinning.

Wallace said, "Hi, Lafferty. How does it feel to be a dangerous outlaw?"

Jeff said, "I always knew he'd come to a bad end."

"I've been mighty near it," Rock answered. "I can tell you this—I sure was glad to see Indian Charlie this morning."

"I've had three talks with Henry Sale," Wallace said. "He's not happy that I'm here and he's not ready to admit that Rock isn't Ringo Lafferty. I asked him to show me proof he had that you were Lafferty, but he told me that such evidence as he had was confidential until you were rearrested and brought to trial. In other words, he ducked showing it to me. He also reminded me that although I was a sheriff in Sawtelle, I had no authority here."

"A nice cooperative gent, huh?"

"No, an uneasy man. I've an idea he doesn't like knuckling down to Chenoweth, but that he doesn't have the guts to do otherwise. I've talked to a dozen other men here in town. The storekeeper, the man at the feed store, the barber, the agent at the stage office, the manager of the bank, and a few more. I told them who I was and why I came here. I said I was satisfied the man they arrested as Lafferty, really was Rock Wesley, and that I meant to prove it. They didn't seem to like what I said any more than Henry Sale did. This is a sick town."

"I know it," Seigel said.

"Maybe it's time to do something about it."

Seigel looked angry. "I'm ready."

"How about the others who live here?"

Jeff said, "I think some would be ready to throw in with us. Not everybody in town has a business to lose. I've spent a lot of time listening to the talk around town. If we could build a few fires in the right places we could set this whole valley aflame."

"Then let's get started," Rock said. "Roy, do you think you could persuade the sheriff to pay us a visit?"

"Not if he knew you were here," Seigel said. "But if he thought he might learn something through coming to my office, he might come. I'll see what I can do."

He stood up, a tall, thin, gaunt man of books. His skin didn't have the tanned, windburned look of these men from Sawtelle, and he didn't dress as they did, or wear a gun. He was not a man of action, yet these range-hardened men were including him in their plans, just as though he belonged, and it gave him a good feeling. He had resented Chenoweth's domination of Modoc as far back as his first few months in town. He had bowed to it ungraciously because there had been nothing else to do, but here, finally, was a chance to stand for what he believed in, with a bare hope of success.

He turned away, heading for the door.

12

Henry Sale was more worried than he wanted to admit. Much of his uneasiness he blamed on Ken Wallace. He had never met Wallace before, but he had heard about him. Wallace was a man with a history. He had been a ranger, had spent a few years as a deputy United States Marshal, had finally settled in Sawtelle. He was reputed to be lightning-fast with his guns, and an implacable foe of the men who rode the back trails. Of course Wallace had no authority here in Modoc, but a man with such a background was always someone to be reckoned with.

Another thing bothered Sale—that a man like Wallace would go to the trouble of coming this far just because someone he knew was in trouble. Spelled out, that meant that in Sawtelle, Rock Wesley was a man of substance and not just another horse rancher.

It was Arne Chenoweth, however, and Chenoweth's attitude that lay heaviest on his mind. He had tried to warn Chenoweth that because of Wallace's presence, they would have to move carefully, but his warning had made no impression at all. "To hell with Wallace," Chenoweth had answered. "If he gets in our way, we'll smash him. You're the sheriff here in Modoc—at least for the present."

Henry Sale walked to the door, stepped outside. He took a look up and down the dark, quiet Main Street. He knew Chenoweth had a couple men posted somewhere in its shadows, on the theory that Wesley might ride back to town, but most of the Arrowhead riders were out searching the range, hoping to trap him somewhere in the hills. And that might happen. If it did, all his worries were for nothing. Wesley's death would then be Chenoweth's responsibility, although more than likely, it never would be reported.

He returned to his desk and sat down, and a few minutes later looked up as Roy Seigel came in. Seigel's appearance put him immediately on guard. The lawyer had never been friendly to Chenoweth.

Sale's greeting reflected none of his apprehension. It was a genial: "Howdy, Roy. What's got you out tonight?"

"Some papers Meg brought me," Seigel said. "She says Rock Wesley gave them to her to keep for him. I've been thinking of turning them over to Ken Wallace, but you ought to at least see them before I do. A couple are right interesting."

The sheriff drummed on his desk with his fingers. Thoughts were clicking through his mind so fast he was a little amazed at his own thinking. It came to him, first of all, that there was something about what Seigel had said that didn't ring true. In spite of that, the thought of any papers belonging to Rock Wesley floating about gripped his attention. Papers could be dangerous things—he had known a scrap of paper to cost a man his life. He had seen another paper which had saved a man from hanging. He knew, suddenly, that he had to see these papers, no matter what they were.

"Let's have them," he said abruptly, stretching out his hand."

"They're in my office safe," Seigel answered. "I didn't want to take a chance of losing them."

"Does Wallace know about them?"

"Not yet."

Sale heaved his bulk erect. "I'm not sold yet on the idea that Wesley's not Lafferty. Wallace could be in cahoots with him. I think I better have a look at those papers, Seigel. Let's go back to your office."

"Remember, I haven't said I'd hand them over to you," Seigel warned.

"We'll talk about that after I've seen them," the sheriff said. "Let's go."

He left the office door open and the lamp still burning, turned low. They walked up the street to Seigel's office. As they stepped inside, Seigel said, "I've moved my safe to the back room," and gestured Sale ahead of him. He threw open the door.

Sale stopped dead at sight of Wallace, Jeff Elliott and Rock Wesley. He knew instantly that he had walked into a trap. He wanted to back away but felt Seigel standing so close behind him that he could not even draw his gun without jostling the lawyer with his elbow, and that would spoil his speed.

With an effort, he reminded himself that he carried the authority of the law in Modoc, and tried to hide the cold fear creeping over his body.

"Hello, sheriff," Rock said. "Pull up a chair. We've got a few matters to discuss with you."

Henry Sale hesitated, but not for long. From the way Rock, Wallace, and Elliott were looking at him, he could see he had no choice in the matter. He walked to the chair Rock had indicated and sat down. As he did so, the pattern of what he must say in the next few minutes became clear in his mind—*Agree to anything. Say anything you have to, to get away. Then find Chenoweth and tell him where Wesley is.*

Rock stared soberly at Henry Sale, then leaned forward. "Sheriff, who am I?"

"Wesley."

"I'm not an outlaw named Ringo Lafferty?"

"From the papers I found in your pocket when I arrested you, I thought you were Lafferty. I'm sure now I was wrong."

"So if you met me now on the street, you wouldn't arrest me."

"Why should I?"

"Fine. Now let's talk about the Temple Hills outlaws. Who are they, sheriff?"

Henry Sale scowled. He shook his head. "We've never been able to ride them down. Who they are, I don't know. It's a rugged country up north of here. We'd need an army to clean it out."

"I doubt it," Rock said. "But we'll let that go for a minute. Are you convinced that the Temple Hills outlaws got away with my Morgan mares?"

"It looked that way to me," Sale said.

"Suppose I found my mares on the Arrowhead range. What would that prove?"

The sheriff moistened his lips. He squirmed in his chair. "I don't know, Wesley," he said finally. "I can't believe you'll find 'em there."

"But if I do, will you lead a posse there to recover them? And will you ask Arne Chenoweth to explain what they're doing on his land?"

Sale brushed his hand over his forehead and was surprised to discover he was perspiring. He glanced at the men facing him around the table. Not one was smiling. Their eyes were rock hard.

"Well, sheriff?"

Henry Sale said strainedly, "In my book, Chenoweth's the same as any other man. If you can give me any proof he's got your mares, I'll go after 'em."

"Good. That was the proper answer," Rock said dryly. Then he glanced at Wallace. "What do you think, Ken?"

"I think we may have a job for the sheriff to do tomorrow," Ken Wallace said.

"And it would be too bad if he wasn't around to handle it."

"Exactly."

Rock looked over at Roy Seigel. He asked, "Roy, where's that barn where you put my horse?"

"Not more than a dozen steps from here," Seigel answered.

"Tell me about it."

"It's just a barn no one's using. A man named Webster used to keep his horse there, but Webster's been gone for months. No one uses the place now. It's on property Carl Blake owns. Blake is the storekeeper. He never goes there."

"Could a man pass the night there?"

"Comfortably."

Henry Sale knew what was coming. He jerked to his feet, his hand sweeping close on his gun. "You can't do this!" he shouted. "I won't stand for it!"

No one at the table moved. No one seemed the least bit startled. There was a moment of silence, before Rock said mildly, "I wouldn't draw that gun if I were you, sheriff. Someone might get hurt. Suppose, instead, you just unbuckle your gunbelt and lay the whole thing on the table."

Henry Sale wanted to yell out his defiance. He glanced at the men facing him. Not one had made a motion to reach for his gun, but he knew how fast Wesley could move and he had heard of the blinding speed of Ken Wallace. The sudden conviction came to him that if he pulled his gun he would be a dead man before he could fire a single shot. His shoulders slumped. After another moment of hesitation he unbuckled his belt and laid it on the table.

"You'll be sorry for this," he rumbled. "As long as you live, you'll regret it."

"Maybe so," Rock said. "But we want you handy when we need you, sheriff. Jeff, you and Roy Seigel walk the sheriff over to the barn and see that he's made comfortable for the night. Use a couple of good, strong lengths of rope."

"Sale never will lead a posse against Chenoweth," Wallace declared after the sheriff had been led away.

"But at least he won't turn on us while he's tied up in the barn," Rock answered. "Figure it any way you want to, Ken, he's the law in Modoc. We don't want him working actively against us."

Rock stood up, stretched, took a brief turn around the room, then returned to the table and fell into a brooding consideration of the problem they faced. He had no doubt but that Indian Charlie would locate the missing mares, and it might not take him very long. But what then? Chenoweth still was a man of power in the valley, and could claim that the mysterious outlaws from the Temple Hills had driven the mares to a pasture on his range. Or he could disclaim all knowledge of how they happened to be found on his place, and who in Modoc would have the courage to say otherwise?

Ken Wallace stirred up the fire in the stove, added water to the coffeepot, then came back to the table. His thoughts must have been running along the same lines, for he said, "Roy Seigel's a man we can count on, and I'll bet he could handle a gun in a pinch. McAlpin, too. And that daughter of his has plenty of fire. If she only wasn't a girl—"

"Like her better that way," Rock said, grinning.

He leaned back in his chair, a little surprised at finding how much he was looking forward to meeting her again in the morning. He never had known a woman who had made quite the impression on him that she had. She had fought with him over his efforts to break Chenoweth's grip on the town and valley, and yet had risked all that a woman can risk to get him out of jail when his case seemed hopeless. He laughed softly at a thought that she would never be satisfied to be the shadow of the man she married. If she had an opinion about something, she would speak up.

Roy Seigel and Jeff Elliott came back from the barn, looking rather pleased. Jeff said, "You know, that's quite a barn back there. It could hold thirty more men besides Henry Sale without crowding."

Rock looked up. "Say that again!"

"Huh?"

Rock was suddenly speculative—he had an idea to work on. The main source of Chenoweth's power lay in the men who rode for him; strip the rancher of their support, or even cut down the number of men he could call on, and . . .

"Are you thinking along the lines I am?" Wallace asked.

Rock grinned. He asked, "How many of Chenoweth's crew are in town?"

"Six or eight. How many would you guess, Seigel?"

"A few more," Seigel said. "I don't know how many have ridden in since dark."

"Do they hang out mostly at the Golden Horseshoe?"

"There, or at the Cattlemen's saloon."

"It's a dark night," Rock said. "Suppose we pick up a few and take them to the barn to keep the sheriff from getting lonely. The more of Chenoweth's men we put out of commission, the less we'll have to worry about."

"Sounds like a good idea to me," Jeff said. "We could start with the two he's got posted, watching the main street. I think they may be on the lookout for you. About an hour ago, one was hanging around near the barber shop. The other was leaning against the stage-yard fence."

Rock stood up. "We'll start with them, Roy, do you want a part in this? It could turn out a little rough."

The attorney rubbed his thin hands together, straightening. "You bet I want a part in it. I'll get my gun."

"Get it."

Roy Seigel took a deep breath as he turned to go to his office. The gun was in his desk. He had never fired it, had bought it to carry on trips out of town. He wondered what he would do tonight if he got into a tight place and had to shoot a man. He decided, bleakly, that in such a case, he would shoot. He got his gun, slipped it into his coat pocket, and rejoined the others.

"Ready," he announced in a firm voice.

Rock turned down the lamp, blew out the flame. They left by the back door.

13

Art Levering didn't like the assignment he had drawn. When he came to town it usually was to enjoy himself, do a little drinking or sit in a poker game. Standing in the deep shadow of the barber shop and watching the almost deserted street for a man he figured was miles away, wasn't his idea of the way to spend the evening. But Bealer Harrison had posted him here, and had insisted the job was damned important, and that there was a real chance Rock Wesley might come riding into town. Sooner or later, if he wasn't trapped out in the hills, he would have to head somewhere for supplies.

That sounded reasonable, of course, if you figured Wesley to be as crazy as some of his actions suggested. Art still didn't like his assignment. He pictured what it was like in the Golden Horseshoe, where a couple games would be going on. By now, with a run of luck, he might have been fifty dollars ahead.

Someone was coming up the street toward him. A big, bulky man. Not Wesley—Wesley was a lot leaner. The momentary warning which had alerted Art Levering faded. He watched with only a casual interest as the bulky man drew nearer, and was only slightly surprised when he stopped and stared at him. Others had passed him without noticing him.

"Howdy, friend," the bulky man said. "You all right? You look mighty lonesome."

"Move along, mister," Levering said harshly.

The bulky man laughed and stepped closer. There was an unlighted cigar in his mouth. He took it out, looked at it, and said. "You don't have a match, do you?"

Alarm reached sharply now into Levering's awareness. He took a step to one side, reaching for his gun. "I told you, mister—"

The big man's gun was out, inches from Art Levering's belly. Art had not even seen the man's hand move.

"Steady!" the man ordered. "One yell out of you, and you're dead."

Levering stood rigid. This man facing him wasn't Wesley. It occurred to him that the gun pointing at him might mean a hold-up, but that didn't seem likely, either—no one ever accused Art Levering of looking like he had enough money to make a hold-up worthwhile.

Footsteps sounded through the shadows back along the building and he took a quick look that way. Three men were approaching. One stepped close to him, took his gun, and ordered, "Come with us, fella. Behave yourself and you won't get hurt."

Levering said, "There'll be hell to pay when Chenoweth—"

One of the men laughed. "You're right about that—there'll be hell to pay. And you'll be mighty lucky not to get caught in the middle of it. We're just putting you away for a while—for safekeeping."

Wild thoughts of making a break pounded through Levering's head, but were quickly discarded. Surrounded by four men he had no chance to escape. Without further argument he went with his captors.

A few moments later he stood near the stage yard, a gun pressed to his back, and watched the four men pick up Chuck Knowles as easily as they had him. The night was not cold, but the sweat on Art Levering's neck and shoulders felt icy.

One of the poker games in the Golden Horseshoe saloon broke up just after midnight, and three of Chenoweth's riders who were the heavy winners and wanted to press their luck, decided they might be able to crowd into the game still in progress at the Cattlemen's saloon. They headed that way down the deserted street.

As they were passing the bank, a man called out to them, "Hey, fellows, what do you think of this?"

They turned and saw that four men had stepped

out on the boardwalk behind them, and that four steady guns covered them. Their hands shot instantly into the air.

Rock Wesley said, "Jeff, you and I'll take their guns. Ken and Roy will keep them covered."

Almost before they realized it, the three men had been disarmed, and were being herded back the way they had come, to stand in the back yard of the Golden Horseshoe. Three guns were held in their backs, while the fourth man patrolled restlessly between the back door of the saloon and the street.

Half an hour later, Lou Markley left the Golden Horseshoe and stepped around behind it to relieve himself. He was standing virtually helpless when the fourth man walked up to him and pressed a gun to his back.

Ordinarily, Arne Chenoweth enjoyed his poker. He played a bullish game. Sometimes he lost, sometimes he won. Usually he came out a little ahead. It wasn't often that he had a night when the cards ran continually against him, but they did tonight. As the hours wore on he grew more and more irritated. Finally, in a burst of anger, he tore the cards he had drawn in half, pushed back his chair, and stood up.

"To hell with it," he grated. "I'll get even tomorrow. Bealer, round up the crew an' get 'em started home."

He went outside, climbed to his horse and pounded out of town, alone. It took him three hours to make it to the Arrowhead and it was near four in the morning when he got to bed.

He was up at six, and he felt stiff, logy, and more tired than he wanted to admit. He kept a room in the hotel in Modoc, and as a rule, stayed in town after a late poker session. He wished now that he had done so the night before. He could have used the sleep, and could have ridden out here this morning to check on the men who were hunting Wesley.

Stuffy Kline, the cook, brought his morning coffee to his desk, and with it a report which didn't make sense. Eight of his men hadn't shown up for breakfast. Stuffy reeled off their names. The eight were men who had been in town the night before. One of the eight was Bealer Harrison.

Chenoweth definitely remembered having told Bealer to get his crew together and get them started home. He couldn't imagine why his order had not been carried out. Only one possibility occurred to him. Before leaving town or on the way here, Bealer and those with him had run across Wesley, or some tip as to where Wesley might be.

"Is Hondo here?" he asked, naming one of the men who had been in town but who had not been mentioned by Stuffy as missing.

The cook nodded.

"Tell him I want to see him," Chenoweth said. "And get Jake Leydon, too."

Leydon and Hondo came in to see him together. Leydon, who had headed the hunt for Wesley the day before, reported no success. The Morgan mares were still safely corralled in a meadow two miles to the south. No strange rider had been near them.

Chenoweth turned to Hondo. "When did you leave Modoc?"

"Near one o'clock, Arne," Hondo replied. "Didn't get much sleep."

"Who rode here with you?"

"Slim, and Cam Hudson."

"Did you see Bealer before you left?"

"Yep. He came to the Cattlemen's and told us to pull out for home. We did."

"Then what happened to Bealer and the others?"

"How the hell should I know?" Hondo shrugged.

Chenoweth took a brief turn around the room. Eight men hadn't returned from town the night before. He could think of only one thing to attribute it to—a report on Wesley. And damn it, it was about time. This whole affair was beginning to wear on his nerves.

"Jake, have the men saddle up," he ordered. "We're leaving for Modoc, right away. Name four to stay here an' put 'em to work on the new well, but tell 'em to keep an eye peeled."

He shaved, then had a hurried breakfast, and by this time felt a little better. Whatever had delayed his men in town, he sensed matters building to a showdown, and a showdown had never frightened him. He had pushed too many himself—and always had dictated the terms.

His first stop in town was the sheriff's office, but Henry Sale wasn't there. The office was locked. Chenoweth sent a man to Sale's home to fetch him, then dropped in at the bank.

"McAlpin been in to see you?" he asked the manager.

"Nope. Not yet," the manager answered.

"Then find him," Chenoweth ordered. "Tell him no more credit goes to him and call in his loans. A man who can't take care of his property isn't a man to be trusted."

"Lots of folks don't like what happened to McAlpin," the bank manager said uneasily. "It might look better if we didn't push him too hard just now."

"Who the hell cares how it looks?" Chenoweth said angrily. "See him today."

He left the bank, crossed to the sheriff's office, and stood waiting there until the man he had sent after the sheriff, returned. The man was alone. He shook his head, looking puzzled. "Henry Sale's not home. His wife said he didn't come in last night and she's worried about him."

"What about his horse?"

"In the barn."

Chenoweth frowned, then shook off his first vague feeling of uneasiness. If things had broken fast last night and a chase had been necessary, the sheriff might have borrowed some other horse. "Scout up and down the street," he suggested. "See if you can find out what happened last night. I'll be in the store. Then I'm going over to the Golden Horseshoe."

He turned down the street to Blake's store and went inside. Several men were standing at the back counter, talking. When they saw him, they fell suddenly silent. He walked forward, nodded, and tried not to show the annoyance he felt.

"I'll take a half-dozen of those cigars you keep for me, Carl," he said to the storekeeper.

Carl Blake got out the box and opened it. Chenoweth scooped out his cigars. He lit one, put the others in his pocket, and glanced at Eddie Carson who was standing next to him. Carson was one of the drivers for the stage line and when not off on a trip usually stayed up as long as anything was open.

"What was the excitement here in town, Eddie?" he asked bluntly.

"Excitement?" Eddie said. "I don't know of any excitement."

"The sheriff's not in town," Chenoweth said.

"He must have gone chasing off somewhere."

"If he did, I don't know anything about it," Eddie said. "What did I miss last night? Any of you other fellows know?"

"I didn't hear of anything unusual," Mike Sloan said.

The others shook their heads.

Chenoweth glanced at Sloan, who ran a clothing store. He looked at the others, Doc Brubaker, Bart Lessor, a rancher from east of town, Sol Weist, the barber. He couldn't read anything in their faces. The uneasiness he had felt a moment before returned. Damn it, something had happened. Something had to have happened. The sheriff was gone. Eight of his men were missing. People didn't just drop out of sight.

He turned angrily toward the door just as someone came in. Against the light from outside he didn't immediately recognize the newcomer, but presently he did. The man was Frank Bradley, Edna's husband. It ran through his mind that Edna might know what had happened. If she did, she would tell him.

He moved on past Bradley with a curt nod, but when the man called his name, he stopped, and looked back, and instantly was aware of a sharp apprehension. Bradley was scowling and the hard look in his eyes was something he almost could feel. As far back as he could remember, no one had looked at him like that. Without knowing it, his hand dropped to his gun.

Bradley stepped toward him, and spoke. His words were low, but each one was clear and distinct. "Chenoweth, keep away from my wife. Keep away from her—or I'll kill you."

Chenoweth rocked back on his heels, his face turning red. Two urgencies swept through him in such rapid succession that their contrary drives left him confused. His first impulse was to sweep up his gun and end Bradley's life but even as that desire hit him he realized that Bradley, who worked as bartender in Long Chance saloon, was not armed, and that not even he could shoot an unarmed man in front of witnesses. He could smash Bradley down with his fists, but there was no telling what the man had found out, and what would come out in a brawl.

He could feel Bradley's eyes burning into his face. His anger let him meet and match the promise of violence that was there.

He said roughly, "I don't know what the hell you're talking about."

"You savvy what I'm talking about," Bradley said. "I said, stay away from my wife."

Chenoweth said, "If you're a man and want to talk like that, wear a gun. When you do, I'll talk to you. I haven't got time to mess around with your kind now."

He turned stiffly and strode out.

Ten minutes later, and with two drinks warming him, he leaned against the bar in the Golden Horseshoe, and promised himself that Bradley would die. But even as he reached the decision, he knew that nothing would be gained by Bradley's death. Edna had been a mistake. He didn't want Edna. He didn't really give a damn about her husband. The one to be angry with was himself.

The man he had sent to make inquiries along the street came in, still looking puzzled, and still shaking his head. "Nobody knows of anything happening last night. Near as I can find out, there wasn't any kind of ruckus at all."

"There had to be," Chenoweth whipped out. "Find Jake Leydon and tell him I want to see him."

He took another drink, went outside and stood looking up and down the street. A wrongness about the town hit him—what had given a man like Bradley the courage to threaten him? What had the men in Blake's store been talking about when he came in, and why had they turned silent at his arrival? And why had the manager of his bank questioned his wisdom in calling McAlpin's loans? Since when had either of them had to worry about what people liked? Maybe it was time to give the town a lesson in deportment.

He saw Meg coming up the street and he waited

until she was near, then pulled off his hat and managed a smile. He said, "Hello, Meg."

She stopped and stood staring at him, the same kind of look in her eyes as he had seen in the eyes of Frank Bradley. "I'm surprised you have the nerve to speak to me after what your men did at our ranch," she answered scornfully.

"But I wasn't responsible for that, Meg," he answered, still smiling. "You've got the Arrowhead all wrong."

"No, I understand you perfectly, Mr. Chenoweth," she answered. "I always have. I never would have married you. For a long time I've been afraid of you—afraid of what you might do, but I'm not afraid of you any longer. You did—or tried to do—your worst. You failed. Right now you're licked and don't know it."

Chenoweth's face darkened. He took a step toward her. "Now look here, Meg—"

"No, you listen to me," Meg said. "We don't want you in Modoc. Get out—while you can."

Chenoweth's mouth dropped open. He was too shocked to make any immediate answer and before he could speak, Meg had walked past him and up the street. He stared after her, wide-eyed, feeling a futile anger. What had given Meg McAlpin the courage to talk to him that way—to threaten him? What was wrong with the town, anyhow?

He slammed his fist into the palm of his hand. By God, before another night could pass, Modoc would get the lesson it needed. He waited impatiently for Jake Leydon.

14

Rock stood guard while Jeff released one of the prisoners in the barn. The man was allowed to care for his personal needs, then was provided with a scanty breakfast, and after this was tied up again.

One after another, the others received the same treatment. They had learned the night before the value of silence. A kerosene lantern, wick turned low, burned dimly on top of a bale of dry hay—they had all been told that at the first sign of a commotion, or concerted shout, the lantern would be kicked over, setting the barn on fire. Before help could arrive, the bound men would certainly perish. They watched each other more carefully than their captors watched them.

When the last man had been cared for, Rock holstered his gun and glanced at Jeff. "Think you can handle them?"

Jeff grinned. "Never did see so many cooperative gents. I don't think I'll have any trouble with them, Rock."

"Then I'll go back to Roy's office," Rock said. "We ought to be hearing from Charlie before long."

The morning was half gone. He had expected Indian Charlie to arrive before this, and hoped to find him at Seigel's when he got there, but was disappointed.

"It may be a week before we hear from him," Seigel said pessimistically. "How many days did you spend on the Arrowhead without finding a trace of your mares?"

"Too many," Rock admitted. "But toward the end I covered most of the land around the ranch house. If the mares are being held where I think they are, Charlie's found them by this time."

"Or he may have run into trouble."

"There's always that."

"I wish he'd get here as much as you do," Seigel said. "We're sitting on a powder keg. I suppose you know it."

"But it can't be helped, Roy."

"No, I suppose it can't," Seigel replied.

Someone rattled the front door. Seigel went to answer it, and a moment later returned, accompanied by Ed McAlpin and Jim Fleming.

"Just got to town a few minutes ago," Fleming said. "Met McAlpin, and heard what's been happening. Could you use another recruit?"

"We could use fifty," Rock said.

"If it came right down to cases, this town would line up to a man on our side. But unless it looks like Chenoweth's cornered, there are a good many who won't want to commit themselves. Still, I know two men I think we can count on."

"In a fight?"

"I believe they'd risk a fight, if they thought there was any chance we might win."

"But that's the problem," Rock said. "How long do you think we'd hold those men in the barn if Chenoweth knew where they were?"

"How've you managed to keep 'em quiet?"

Rock told him about the bale of hay and the lantern, and Fleming grinned. "That's talking their language. 'Course I know you wouldn't burn helpless men, but they would— and so they think you would." Fleming glanced at McAlpin. "Let's see what we can do."

"I'm ready," McAlpin nodded. "I know a few men myself we can talk to."

The two went out. Ken Wallace came in to report that Chenoweth was in town. "He brought quite a crowd with him, too," Wallace said. "More men than we could handle, right now. I'll go back, keep an eye on 'em."

He left again.

Seigel busied himself in his office, to maintain an appearance of normalcy. Alone in the back room, Rock Wesley stretched out on the attorney's cot, and tried to control his urgencies. He needed two things. Definite word from Indian Charlie as to where the Morgan mares were being held, and after that, a crew to support him when he faced Chenoweth. Perhaps it could be worked so that Chenoweth could be arrested before his men got word of what was going on. If his men were left without leadership, a fight might be avoided.

He heard voices from the front room—a few moments later, Meg appeared in the doorway. She was frowning, as always when they met. Rock grinned at her and stood up. He was beginning to like even her frown.

"Roy told me what happened last night," she said. "How long do you suppose it will be before Arne Chenoweth learns about your holding his men."

Rock shrugged. "Who knows? Ten minutes, an hour, a day."

"And what do you think he'll do when he finds out?"

"Come after them if he's not in jail."

"And how would you get to him to arrest him? I saw six of his men on the street as I walked here. Rock, what you're doing frightens me."

"Me, too," Rock said. "A fight is never anything not to worry about. But neither is it anything to leave unfinished." He pulled out a chair for her. "Sit down and have some coffee."

She sat down, but shook her head to coffee. "I met Chenoweth on the street on my way here. I wasn't very kind in what I said to him. Rock, there are times I wish I was a man."

"I can't go along with that," Rock said, grinning. "What will you do after all this is over?"

"Help father rebuild the ranch. Maybe we can recover some of the cattle he lost."

"Do you like it here?"

"Very much."

"You'd like Sawtelle, too, and the high mesa country."

She looked directly at him. "Yes, I think I would."

He hadn't expected this answer and was momentarily confused, but he reached out and covered her hand with his, and said, "Meg, I'd like to show it to you. It isn't mountain land. It's flat but wooded in many places and the mountains are all around us, some high and snow-covered most of the year. There's no place in the West like the high mesa country."

Meg didn't pull her hand away. She wasn't looking at him now. She seemed to have found something on the wall to stare at. Her face had a warm color in it. Rock felt suddenly sure of himself, confident of what he wanted. He laughed softly and said, "We wouldn't fight all the time, Meg. Just part of the time."

A smile tugged at her lips. She pulled her hand away. "You have other things on your mind right now."

"What's more important?" Rock asked. "Why don't we—"

Loud voices reached them from the front room. One was Roy Seigel's. The other, Rock didn't recognize. He heard the sounds of a scuffle, and of a thud as someone fell; then footsteps were moving toward the rear door.

He came quickly to his feet, reaching out to pull Meg erect and push her almost roughly toward the far side of the room. He was reaching for his gun when the door slammed open and Tom Garmish stepped into the room.

Rock's hand paused in midreach. A trickle of blood showed at the corner of Tom's mouth, an indication that Roy Seigel had managed to get in at least one blow before he had been downed. But it was a blow which apparently hadn't bothered Garmish; in his eyes, as he stared at Rock Wesley, was a triumphant look. Here, at last, was the man he had promised to find—no matter what the outcome of their meeting might be, he had that small measure of satisfaction—he had found Rock Wesley for Chenoweth.

He didn't glance at Meg who had staggered against the wall and was leaning there, her body rigid. He probably didn't notice she was in the room. He saw no one but Rock. He was breathing noisily and his right hand was only inches from his holstered gun.

His lips moved, and his words came out in a grating whisper. "Wesley, I don't have my slicker on, this time. I can get at my gun. Like this!"

His hand whipped down and up, clawing his gun from its holster. Rock drew and fired. He felt the sting of a bullet scraping his arm. He fired again as Garmish took a backward step. The man turned half around, then suddenly collapsed.

Rock threw a quick look at Meg McAlpin. She was still leaning against the wall. Her face showed no color at all. She looked at the body of Tom Garmish, slumped in the doorway, then looked at Rock, her eyes wide and glassy.

"I'm sorry, Meg," he said thickly. "There wasn't anything else I could do."

Stepping quickly to the door, he stared into the front room. The crowd of the curious that would gather here, attracted by the shooting, hadn't yet shown up, but he knew he didn't have much time. Roy Seigel was again on his feet, near the center of the room. He held one hand against his jaw. He seemed shocked, bewildered.

Rock called. "Roy, how well can you lie?"

The attorney looked at him. "As well as the next man, I suppose."

"Then come here and get my gun. Tell whoever comes that you were showing Meg how well you could shoot and that the shots they heard were fired from the back door at a target. Hurry. We haven't much time."

The attorney came forward. Rock handed him his gun, then stooped and picked up the weapon Garmish had dropped. It was the same make and caliber as his own. He slid it into his holster and said, "Try to keep anyone from coming back here, if you can. Meg, get in the front room."

He pushed her into the front room and closed the door not an instant too soon. As he turned away from it he heard the voices of those who were gathering out front.

It took him less than a minute to thrust the body of Tom Garmish under the bunk, out of sight, and to mop up the trail of blood across the floor. He wrapped his kerchief around the bullet-crease in his arm and opened the back door.

The barn was twenty steps away. He had made them twice this morning, and apparently without being noticed, but this time the danger would be greater. Men probably were converging on the attorney's office from every direction. Still, he would have to chance it. To remain where he was would be even more risky. Some who came to Seigel's office might not believe what the attorney would say. Chenoweth or one of his men might be overly suspicious and insist on a look in the back room.

He took a deep breath, then moved quickly toward the barn, fighting down the impulse to run. To run would be to invite attention, a second look from a chance witness. He reached the barn door, pulled it open and slid inside, then leaned against it weakly.

Jeff Elliott asked, "What happened, Rock?"

"Trouble."

Jeff shrugged philosophically. "What else?"

Rock had to grin at that. "Trouble is all," he said. He turned and took a look at their prisoners. "No excitement here?"

Jeff said, "We heard the shots. Since you're here, these fellers figure to have lost another friend. Who was it this time?"

Rock said in a troubled voice, "Tom Garmish. He pulled on me, left me no choice. What bothers me is that he busted into Roy's place, looking for me. Chenoweth might be getting warm."

Jeff asked, "You didn't ask him how come he guessed you were there?"

"Didn't have time."

Jeff shook his head. "Rock, you ought to learn not to plug 'em dead center like that the first shot. A dead man is practically worthless when you want information. Tell you what—we get home, I'm gonna give you some lessons."

The barn had grown deathly still, except for Jeff's easy, droning voice—the eight prisoners seemed totally absorbed in what he had to say.

Jeff now looked them over. " 'Course, we could practice a little on these fellers right there."

Rock had to grin again. "They been giving you a hard time?"

"Naw—quietest little bunch of babes in the woods I ever did see. 'Course, I had to knock a coupla heads when the shooting started, but mostly they just whimper a little at meal times, or when they need their diapers changed."

Gradually Jeff's casual chatter began to have its intended effect on Rock—he felt the tension attendant on his duel with Tom Garmish start to drain out of him. He moved to a corner of the barn, where a crack in the boards afforded him a limited view of the street, between two buildings.

A man showed up suddenly from between the feed store and the barber shop. He stopped, tilted back his hat, and took time to light the cigarette he had rolled. It was Jim Fleming. After lighting the cigarette, he began to drift across the street.

"Fleming is headed this way," Rock called.

Near the door, Jeff Elliott nodded. He eased the door open a crack. Fleming came in. "Nice and quiet in here," he said, grinning. "Your prisoners must like it."

Jeff said, "They never had it easier."

"What happened at Seigel's a few minutes ago?" Rock asked.

"Roy took a few practice shots through the back door. He wanted to show Meg how well he could shoot. At least, that's what he said. Meg backed him up." Fleming paused, then said, "Now, what really happened? I didn't get the chance to ask."

"Garmish showed up. He pulled his gun on me. His body's in the back room, under the bunk."

Fleming whistled. "That was a close one. What I came here to tell you was this. Indian Charlie's back. He's found your mares. They're on the

Arrowhead, penned up in a narrow valley not two miles south of the ranch house."

Rock felt as though a great weight had fallen from his shoulders. He had worried about Charlie. "Where's Charlie now?"

"On the hotel porch, with Ken Wallace. They want to know what to do. Wallace says he's ready to go out on a limb and place Chenoweth under arrest, but he'll need a crowd to back him up, if he tries it."

"How many can we count on?"

"Give me half an hour, and I'll round up at least six who will go along with us. Ed McAlpin and I talked to that many during the past hour. They're all for us. They want to see Chenoweth smashed, but until now we didn't have anything to tell them that they could get their teeth into."

Rock nodded. With half a dozen men to cover him, Wallace could step up to Chenoweth, disarm him and throw him in jail before the rest of his men or the rest of the town of Modoc knew what was going on. He didn't have the authority for a step like that, but could assume it, and now could produce the evidence necessary to make the arrest stick. They might even be able to get Henry Sale to go along with them.

As he was turning this over in his mind, Jeff called out from the corner of the barn, a note of alarm in his voice. Rock hurried over.

"Look outside," Jeff said. "At the far corner

of Seigel's office, then at the rear of the next building."

Rock peered through the crack in the boards. At first he saw nothing unusual, but as he watched he saw a man ease to the back corner of Seigel's office, to study the barn. The man carried a rifle. An instant later another man, similarly armed, appeared at the back corner of the next building.

Jeff had pulled the barn door slightly open and was looking in the other direction. "We're covered from the north, too, Rock," he called. "I can see three men up that way. It seems as though Chenoweth's got things figured out. We're pinned down."

Rock made no answer, but he knew that what Jeff had said was true. Indian Charlie had returned too late, by maybe an hour. Chenoweth had learned what was happening, and was ready to hit back. The nice, neat plan to place him under arrest was not going to work.

"It looks as though we've got a fight on our hands, doesn't it?" Fleming said. He drew his gun, checked it, then glanced at Rock. "What do you want me to do?"

"Sorry you're caught in this, Jim."

Fleming shrugged. "Reckon I asked for it. I'm not sorry I'm here. Just tell me what to do."

"Take the far corner of the barn—and wait," Rock said. "I imagine we'll be hearing from Chenoweth before long."

He hunkered down on his heels, filled and lit his pipe, and again took a look through the crack in the boards. The men he had spotted a few moments before were still there. He sucked on his pipe, scowling, reflecting that if Indian Charlie had arrived an hour earlier, or if the men Fleming and McAlpin had talked to had had more spirit, things might have worked out differently. Now, it was hard to predict just what lay ahead.

15

The man who had told Chenoweth of the prisoners in the old, vacant barn back of Seigel's office, was Russ Elders, whose ranch bordered on the Arrowhead, and who knew he was open to a raid by the "Temple Hills Outlaws" any time Chenoweth felt like it. He had been approached by McAlpin and Fleming, and had seemed to agree to what they wanted, but the more he thought about it, the more hopeless the venture seemed. No handful of men could stand up to Arrowhead manpower. And it seemed the wise thing for him to do was to take what personal advantage he could from the situation.

He had his talk with Chenoweth, and afterwards, had two stiff drinks in the Long Shot saloon. The drinks, however, didn't wash out of his mouth the bad taste that was there. He tried two more, but two more didn't help. He ordered another.

"If you're in with us," Bradley told him in a growling voice, "you'd better go easy on this stuff."

Elders didn't bother to answer but he assured himself that if Frank Bradley represented the type of man Fleming and McAlpin were choosing, he had done the right thing in talking to Chenoweth. Bradley was no fighting man.

But even this consideration didn't make him feel better; he finished his fifth drink and left the saloon. His horse was tied in front of Blake's store. He walked to it, and was untying it when Jinny Blake came out on the hotel porch.

"Not leaving town, are you, Russ?" she asked surprised.

"Gotta get home," Elders mumbled.

"But you told Jim—"

He shook his head. "Gotta get home. Got things to do."

He pulled himself into the saddle and headed out of town.

Jinny watched him leave, then turned abruptly, and marched back into the store. "How much does Russ Elders owe us?" she asked her father.

"Maybe three hundred dollars," Carl Blake said.

"He gets no more credit," Jinny said. "Not a cent. He just left town."

Blake frowned, stood silent a moment. At last he said, "Maybe he was wise, Jinny. What do we know of these men from Sawtelle? What chance have they got against Arne Chenoweth?"

"None, if we all ride out of town," Jinny said. "You're not weakening, too, are you?"

He looked at her, then looked away, shifting uneasily on his feet. "It's sometimes hard to know what's the right thing to do. We don't live in a perfect world, Jinny. If Arne Chenoweth has done something wrong, he should be punished. But for men to take the law into their own hands—"

"The law!" Jinny flared. "Does Henry Sale represent the law, or does he represent whatever Chenoweth wants? I believe in law, but in law that's fair to everyone."

She turned angrily away and went outside again. From across the street, Jim Fleming waved to her. Her eyes brightened. She waved back, and half expected him to come over and talk to her for a minute, but he didn't. Instead, he turned between two of the buildings and disappeared from sight. It struck her that maybe he was on his way to the barn where Chenoweth's men were being held prisoner. This gave her a strange thrill of pride and she admitted to herself what she had known the day before—that she was in love with him again. Jim, suddenly, had become the kind of man she once had dreamed him . . . a man of conviction and courage.

But the smile on her face didn't stay there very long. Two of Chenoweth's men, coming up the street, turned down the passageway through which Jim had walked. Another turned down the passageway between Seigel's and the barber shop. Fear struck through her. It was an icy, numbing fear that seemed to paralyze her limbs. She looked up and down the street. On the hotel porch, four of Chenoweth's men stood grouped around Ken Wallace. One seemed to be saying something to him. And after a moment Wallace stood up, surrendered his gun, and walked up the street with the men to the sheriff's office. The entire group went inside.

What did it mean? Jinny brushed back her hair. She looked toward the passageway into which Jim had disappeared, only to be followed a few minutes later by two of Chenoweth's men. She was listening—listening acutely—for the sound of shots. A prayer was running through her mind...

"Hello, Jinny," said a voice near her.

She twisted her head and found herself looking at Arne Chenoweth, and she noticed, instantly, how confident he looked, how completely sure of himself.

"Nice day, isn't it?" Chenoweth continued. "And it's to be a great day for Modoc—a day when some of the people around here learn better than to put their trust in strangers. I hope no friends of yours are among those who will have to be arrested."

"Arrested?" Jinny said. "But the sheriff—"

"I just talked to Sol Maxwell, the only other county commissioner besides myself who's in town. As an emergency measure, we've appointed Jake Leydon as sheriff. He's already made his first arrest, and locked up a man who calls himself Ken Wallace, but who probably is one of the Lafferty band of outlaws. We expect to get our hands on Lafferty himself before much longer. He's holed up in that old vacant barn, back of Seigel's. I'd stay off the streets if I were you. There may be some shooting before he surrenders."

Jim was in that barn. She wanted to beg Chenoweth not to start shooting, but she knew he wouldn't listen to her. Nor would Jim want her to beg anything from Chenoweth. As she realized this, her head came up proudly and from somewhere she felt a surge of courage. Words came to her, and she spoke them.

"Mr. Chenoweth, do you remember Arch Latham? Every time he came to town and saw Joe Wadleigh's dog, he used to kick it, and the dog would slink away. Joe took it like the dog did. Joe was afraid of Latham. But one day when Latham came to town and kicked Joe Wadleigh's dog, the dog turned on him and sunk his teeth into the calf of Latham's leg. The bite was enough to put Latham to bed for days. He swore he would kill the dog and when he could ride again he came to town to do it. What happened? Joe Wadleigh met him and killed him. I agreed with what you said earlier. This is going to be a great day for Modoc. The people who live here are tired of being kicked around."

"By me?" Chenoweth asked, his face dark with anger.

"Yes, by you."

He took a step toward her, and for a moment Jinny thought he meant to strike her. But he didn't. He lowered the arm he had half lifted, brushed on by her, and angled toward Seigel's.

Jinny took a deep breath, then followed him.

Arne Chenoweth's anger still was with him as he got to Seigel's. He pushed open the door, stepped inside. Three people were there. Meg McAlpin, her father, and the attorney. In the sharp way they looked at him he thought he could read apprehension. This made him feel better. It was high time folks around here learned to respect him again.

"You three are in trouble," he said gruffly. "I've just learned what happened last night. I'm sure you were in on it. Seigel, and I suspect Meg and her father were. Am I right?"

Roy Seigel surprised himself by his blunt answer. "Are you, Chenoweth? I don't know. It could be we don't understand what you're talking about."

The door opened again and Jinny Blake entered.

Chenoweth looked around at her, scowling. "What are you doing here?"

"Aren't you forgetting whose office this is?" Seigel asked. "Jinny's welcome any time."

The cattleman wrenched back to stare at Seigel. There were ugly lines in his face. "You talk too damned much," he grated. "But all your talking, and all your friends won't get you out of the trouble you're in now. Sheltering and helping an outlaw, and kidnapping men who were searching for him, are serious offenses. Just how serious, you'll find out."

Seigel rubbed his thin, bony hands together. A provoking smile showed on his lips. "When?"

"Right now!" Chenoweth shouted.

He went to the door and looked up the street. Jake Leydon and the three men accompanying him were only a few steps away. Chenoweth drew back into the room as they came in. He pointed at Seigel and Ed McAlpin. "There are your next two prisoners. They are charged with helping Ringo Lafferty, and with kidnapping. Lock them up."

Ed McAlpin, who up to this time hadn't said a word, made a desperate grab for his gun. It was only half out of its holster when Leydon's bullet caught him in the chest. He reeled backward as Leydon fired again. McAlpin doubled over as he pitched to the floor.

Meg didn't realize she had screamed, or how swiftly she rushed to her father's side. She knelt down beside him, then sat down, and took his head in her lap. One of the men who had come in with Leydon, stooped over them, then straightened up and said McAlpin was dead, but Meg hadn't needed to hear his words to know it.

Dry, gasping sobs were shaking her body. She made no effort to smother them.

"All right, leave him here. The girls, too," Chenoweth ordered. "Take Seigel to jail and lock him up."

She didn't hear what Seigel said, or hear the men leave, but after a while she realized Jinny was crouching at her side, and that Jinny's arm was around her shoulders.

She looked up, wearily, her face tear-streaked, the lines in it seeming deeper. "He didn't have a chance," she whispered. "Not against a man like Jake Leydon. Why did he try to draw his gun?"

"I don't know, Meg," Jinny answered. "Sometimes we never can understand why things happen the way they do. Maybe he was too tired of backing down to be able to do it again. Maybe he had to prove to himself he wasn't afraid."

Meg looked down into her father's face, remembering the concern she had often seen there when she had been much younger. She started crying again, but after a moment stopped and eased her father's head and shoulders to the floor, and stood up.

"It's about all over, isn't it?" Jinny said.

"What's about all over?"

"The fight against Arne Chenoweth. Ken Wallace and Roy Seigel are in jail. By this time, the barn is surrounded. The men in it will have to surrender."

"They won't," Meg said. "That is, Rock won't."

"Jim is with him."

"Yes. He went there to tell him Indian Charlie was back."

"Indian Charlie?"

Meg nodded. She was surprised to find that her mind suddenly was clear, and working again. She looked at Jinny. "Did you see Ken Wallace arrested?"

"Yes. Four men walked up to him on the hotel porch. They took his gun and marched him to the jail."

"An Indian was on the porch with him. Was the Indian arrested?"

"I don't think so. At least, not while I was watching."

"Then he'll get them out. Maybe it isn't all over, Jinny."

She could see a faint ray of hope in the picture. She remembered Wallace saying to the Indian, "You come along with me, Charlie. Before the day's over, I may need you." Exactly what Wallace had meant by that, she didn't know, but she didn't think he would have surrendered so easily if he hadn't had some plan or other for getting out of jail. Her thoughts switched to the barn. There were only three men to hold the barn against the crowd Chenoweth could throw against them.

"Jinny?" she said abruptly.

"What?"

"Can you fire a gun?"

"Of course I can fire a gun."

"But will you?"

"What do you mean?"

"The barn is surrounded—there isn't a man in town who could get there. But two women could, Jinny. Two women could walk right up to the barn and step inside. Chenoweth's men may be a hard lot, but they wouldn't shoot at—us."

Jinny's eyes had widened. She suddenly was breathing faster.

"Meg," Jinny said, straightening. "Jim's there. I'm going with you."

"We'll use the back door," Meg said.

Meg took another look at the silent figure lying at her feet. She wondered if she would ever see him again.

16

Those in the barn heard the shots that killed Ed McAlpin, but they had no way even of guessing at what had happened. Rock Wesley, from the corner of the barn, kept his eyes glued on the back entrance to the attorney's office, hoping for a glimpse of Meg, that would assure him she was all right. Or a glimpse of Roy Seigel.

"You know what time it is, Rock?" Jeff called.

"Noon. Seems much later than that."

"It's going to be a long day," Rock answered.

Or would it be? How many hours could they hold out against a determined assault by Chenoweth's men. He took another look through the barn. Unused for some time, it had been cleared of everything of value. There wasn't much here to afford them shelter when the firing began.

He glanced back at Seigel's, and felt a sudden relief. Meg was still safe. She stood in the open rear door. Jinny Blake was with her. Suddenly Rock caught his breath. Both women had stepped outside and were walking straight toward the barn.

"Meg! Jinny!" he shouted. "Keep away from here!"

They acted as though they hadn't heard him. A shot from somewhere kicked up dust at their feet but they didn't slow down or turn back. Another shot whistled above their heads, but didn't stop them.

Rock hurried to the barn door. He pulled it open just as Meg and Jinny reached it. A bullet whined through the open door before he could slam it shut. He grabbed the women and rushed them to another part of the barn as two more shots made ragged holes in the door.

"Meg, this barn is entirely surrounded."

"We know it."

"And do you think that because you're here, Chenoweth will go any easier on us?"

"Probably not."

"Then why—"

"I can handle a gun, Rock. So can Jinny."

Rock stared at her, shaking his head numbly.

"I'm afraid you're going to have to put up with us," Meg said. "Where can we be of most help?"

Fleming came toward them, staring uneasily at Jinny. He said, "Jinny, you shouldn't have come here."

"I wanted to be with you," Jinny answered honestly.

"It's what I've wanted too," Fleming said gravely. "But not this way."

He looked helplessly at Rock. "What'll we do with them?"

"You look after Jinny. When things start happening, stay down, close to the ground. We'll hear from Chenoweth before much longer. Meg, you come with me."

He walked back to his post in the corner of the barn, Meg following him. He could no longer see the two men through the crack in the boards, but he was pretty sure they hadn't gone away. He crouched to the ground. Meg dropped down near him.

"I didn't mean to growl at you when I met you at the door," he said slowly. "I just meant that you shouldn't have come here."

She said quietly, "Rock, father's dead."

He stared at her, feeling suddenly helpless.

She went on: "Chenoweth came to Roy's office. Then four of his men came in. One, Jake Leydon, was supposed to have been appointed temporary sheriff. Chenoweth ordered him to arrest father and Roy Seigel. Father reached for his gun and Jake Leydon shot him."

Rock reached for her hand, squeezed it. He said, "Meg, I can't tell you how sorry I am. I was growing to have a real respect for your father."

"They took Roy to jail," Meg continued. "Before that, they arrested Ken Wallace."

"And Charlie?"

"No, I don't think they arrested Indian Charlie."

"Then they made a mistake, Meg, unless they've posted a heavy guard at the jail. Ken and Roy won't be there very long. Charlie'll get them out."

"I thought he might," Meg nodded, and smiled for the first time since entering the barn. "That Indian Charlie must be quite a person."

"He's someone you can depend on," Rock said. "Give Charlie a job to do, and he does it, I don't care how tough. And he doesn't waste time about it, either. You'll grow to love him, as I do."

"If we come through this alive."

Rock shifted his position, moving a little closer to Meg. They both fell silent then, simply sitting and waiting.

"Lafferty!" someone shouted. "Lafferty, we know you're in that barn. We've got men all around it. Come out with your hands in the air."

Rock didn't answer—beside him, he felt Meg stiffen. He had been waiting for some such order as a signal that Chenoweth was ready to close in.

The shout reached him again. "Lafferty, this is your last chance! Walk out while you can."

Rock was still silent. From the lack of firing, he had an idea of what was to come, and had made tentative plans to meet the actual ultimatum. The sheriff, and some of Arne Chenoweth's men were here, and two women had come to the barn, but he doubted that Chenoweth would let them stand in his way. Well, two could play that game.

"Rock!" Jeff Elliott called. "They're rolling a light wagon into the alley. There's a barrel in it, and straw packed around the barrel. They've built a wooden shield over the shafts."

Rock stood up. He hurried to where Jeff was kneeling and peered through a crack in the boards. The wagon was just as Jeff had described it. Light, and with a wooden shield over the shafts, behind which two men could guide it. There was a barrel in the wagon's bed and around it a packing of dry straw.

"Oil in the barrel?"

"What else?" Jeff said. "They're not sending us water. They'll set the straw on fire and crash the wagon against the barn. In another ten minutes this place will be a blazing inferno. What about the men we've got tied up?"

"Untie their legs. Run a rope through their wrist bindings to keep 'em together. Hold 'em where they are until the wagon hits the barn."

Jeff hurried away and as he left, Meg joined Rock. She took a look through a chink in the boards and he heard her catch her breath, and whisper, "It's moving, Rock. They've set the straw on fire."

He had noticed that himself. Chenoweth was giving him no time to think things over. The wagon was already rolling down the slight grade toward the barn, propelled by men holding its shafts and protected by the wooden shield. Rock drew his gun. He aimed six shots, one after another, at that wooden shield, but it was merely a gesture, the wagon rolled on. He stood, pulled Meg to her feet, and started reloading his gun.

He knew exactly what was going to happen in another fraction of a minute. The wagon would crash into the barn and the shock of the crash would splash oil against the wall. A sheet of flame would shoot up to the roof and start spreading. The heat and smoke would make it impossible for anyone to remain in here very long. He and Jeff and Jim Fleming were going to have to make a break for the buildings lining the main street. But the men they had been holding here were going to have to get away too, and he had his plans for them. He wondered if he could count on one thing—that Chenoweth's men would not fire on two women.

He finished reloading his gun, dropped it in its holster and took Meg's arm. He said, "Meg, stick by—not too close to me."

The crash of the wagon into the back wall of the barn interrupted him. A part of the wall buckled with a splintering sound. The entire building shook under the impact. Flames shot into the air, licking up the inside wall and curling toward the loft. The prisoners started shouting. Some, already on their feet, tried to break for the door.

Rock called out rapid orders at Jeff, Jim Fleming, Meg and Jinny. Jeff moved the prisoners to the door and Rock threw the door open, leaped back.

Down the alley, facing the barn door in a wide, half circle, were close to a dozen men—

Chenoweth's men, rifles already at their shoulders.

He yelled, "No shooting—unless you want to hit your own men. We're coming out. The first man who fires a gun is—"

A gun went off. One of the prisoners lurched and swore. Another shot—and Rock yelled at Jeff to turn them loose.

He felt his own gun bucking in his hand as he watched the freed prisoners scatter, and realized he had lost his first gamble. Chenoweth was not a man who would stop at cutting down a friend to get at an enemy. Behind him, in the shadows of the barn, Jeff and Jim Fleming also were firing.

The last of the prisoners reached shelter; Chenoweth's men drew out of sight—the firing died to sporadic single shots. The barn was filling with hot, black smoke. The back wall and half the roof were now on fire, and the heat was growing intense.

Rock said softly, "Meg—you and Jinny clear out. They won't shoot you—"

Used as he was to their disagreeing, he was shocked by the angry rebellion that showed in her face. "No—we're in this together."

He looked past her toward the men outside, and above the crackling of the flames he heard a new sound of gunfire. One of Chenoweth's men stumbled from hiding, dropped to the ground. Another. Then suddenly men were running and firing in confusion and he heard someone shouting and recognized the voice of Ken Wallace. Indian Charlie had not been idle nor had he wasted much time in whatever he had done to get Wallace free.

"Back up, you men. Clear out!" Wallace ordered. "We're taking over."

There was more shooting. Another of Chenoweth's men pitched to the ground. The others broke suddenly for the protection of the nearby buildings, to be met by more gunfire from beyond.

"Now!" Rock shouted. "Break for Seigel's office."

He heard a shot and saw Fleming, who was running ahead of him, stagger, but catch his stride and hurry on, Jinny, at his side, throwing an anxious look at him. He heard another shot, and felt a stinging pain strike across his shoulders. It was like the lash of a whip. He glanced at Meg, and cried, "Hurry, Meg. Get ahead of me. We can't go through the door together."

Twenty steps—twenty long steps. Jeff was inside, then Fleming, stumbling, and with Jinny trying to hold him up. Then Meg, and then he was inside, but almost too weak with relief to stand erect. He found a wall and leaned against it, Meg joining him there, and looking up at him anxiously. Jeff had closed the door. Fleming was sitting on the floor, holding his side, his face twisted with pain. Jinny knelt beside him.

Someone came in the front door from the street and headed toward the back room. Rock drew his gun, swung to face the door, then put the gun away when Ken Wallace came in. Wallace looked well-pleased with himself.

"A close one, huh?" he asked, smiling.

"Too close for comfort. Where's your army?"

"There's only two more in it," Wallace confessed. "Roy Seigel and Charlie. We had a couple of drifters Sale had locked up for drunkenness with us for a while, but they hightailed it soon's things were in hand. They figured this for a loco town."

Roy Seigel looked in from the front room. His hair stood on end and there was a scratch across his cheek, but his eyes held the same look as Wallace's.

"Jail sure agrees with me," he announced. "I'd recommend it for all lawyers."

"Charlie's guarding the front door," Wallace said. "Chenoweth's getting his men together, down the street. By this time, he's figured out what happened. This isn't over yet."

"But they can't run any fire wagon into this place," Rock said. "Ken, take a look at Fleming. He's been hurt."

The sheriff from Sawtelle knelt down at Fleming's side and Rock stepped into the front room. He joined Charlie near the door, put his arm around the Indian's shoulder, and asked, "How goes it, Charlie?"

"I found the mares," Charlie said. "We should take them and go home."

"We will," Rock said. "Maybe tomorrow. But we've got a job to do here first."

He glanced up and down what he could see of the street. No one was in sight. He thought, *Chenoweth can't wait long. He can't let us get away with this, and expect to go on running things in the Modoc Valley. He's got to come after us, and this time he'll have the real authority of Henry Sale to back him up. It puts us in the wrong.*

That was a fact which couldn't be dodged. Chenoweth's man or not, Sale still was the duly elected sheriff.

Meg came up to them. She said, "Hello, Charlie," and then, "Jim was hit through the side. Mr. Wallace says it isn't serious, but it looks serious to me. We ought to have a doctor."

"Then tell Jinny I want to see her."

Meg returned a moment later with Jinny. There were tears in Jinny's eyes, but behind them lay anger.

"Jinny," Rock said. "Ken's seen lots of bullet wounds. If he says it isn't serious, it isn't serious, but it wouldn't hurt any to have a doctor look at it. I still don't think Chenoweth would dare shoot at a woman. Do you want to see if you can get a doctor?"

"Yes," Jinny said instantly.

"And will you do something for us?"

"What?"

"Tell your father, and anyone else you can, that the Morgan mares that were stolen from me are being held on Arrowhead land, close to Arne Chenoweth's ranch house. We're ready to lead a posse there to prove it, and we're going to stay in town and fight it out until we can. And until we see Arne Chenoweth locked up in jail."

Jinny's eyes flashed. "Don't worry. I'll say plenty, and to everyone I see."

She stepped out on the street and cut across it, angling toward Doc Brubaker's.

Rock walked to where Meg was standing. She pointed to the floor near Seigel's desk. "That's where father's body was lying. They've taken him away."

"We'll find out where, when all this is over," he said.

He put his arm around her and she leaned against him, and he stood looking past her, at the street, wondering how soon Chenoweth would make his next move.

17

Doc Brubaker finished dressing the leg of the last of the four wounded men who had been carried to his office. He then turned to Jinny, who had been waiting impatiently. "All right," he nodded. "We'll take care of your man now."

He checked the medical supplies and bandages in his bag, then started up the street with her. Men stood grouped in front of the Golden Horseshoe, listening to Arne Chenoweth, but when Chenoweth saw Brubaker he broke off what he was saying. Jinny never had seen him looking more angry.

"Where the hell do you think you're going?" he asked.

"To take care of another wounded man," Brubaker said.

"Who?"

It was Jinny who answered, almost defiantly. "Jim Fleming."

Chenoweth made an angry motion with his arm. "Forget it for a while. Pretty soon you're going to have a few more up the street who will need your attention."

Brubaker stiffened. "When a man's been hurt—any man —I don't forget it."

He moved on ahead, Jinny at his side. For a

moment Chenoweth stood blocking their way, but as they reached him, he stepped back. "I'll remember this, Brubaker," he said darkly.

"Remember it when you get hurt and need me," Brubaker said.

They walked on.

Chenoweth stared after them, scowling, then swung around to face Henry Sale who stood nearby. "All right, Henry, get started," he ordered. "I want every able-bodied man in this town lined up behind us when we close in on Lafferty at Seigel's. There's no reason we should have to carry the full load. We'll start things. Pin them down where they are. But when it comes to moving in on them, the bigger the crowd we have, the quicker it'll be over."

"I'll see what I can do," Sale mumbled.

"Don't just see what you can do," Chenoweth snapped. "I want results."

Sale started up the street. He found no one in the stage office, and only the bartender in the Texas saloon. The hotel lobby was deserted. The front door of Wybel's store was closed and locked. The saddle shop was empty. He tried Blake's expecting to find it deserted, but there were a dozen or fifteen men in Blake's, and the way they turned to stare at him when he came in made him feel suddenly uneasy. He didn't know what to say, so he said nothing.

Someone spoke up, and he noticed with a start of surprise that it was Frank Bradley, who was the bartender at the Long Chance saloon, and who didn't carry any weight at all in Modoc. From the way he was talking, however, he seemed to think he was more than a bartender.

"We're glad you came here, sheriff," Bradley said. "There are some questions some of us want to ask you."

"Questions?" Sale asked.

"Yes, questions. As we understand it, Chenoweth is holding fifteen stolen Morgan mares in a meadow close to his ranch house. What are you going to do about it?"

"This is the first I've heard about it," Sale said cautiously. "Off-hand, I'd say I didn't believe it, but if it's true, why I'd—I'd treat Chenoweth same as any other man."

"That's what we wanted to hear," Bradley nodded. "Some of us are ready to ride out there with you and see if it's true. Suppose we go right now."

Henry Sale felt a moment of panic. He shook his head. "We've got something else to do first. Lafferty—"

Carl Blake spoke up. "The man you call Lafferty says his name is Wesley. He proved to the McAlpins that's who he was when they found him wounded. Where's your proof that he's an outlaw?"

"The letters I found on him when I arrested him. His papers."

Fred Brady stepped forward. "My sister-in-law, Meg McAlpin, saw the papers he carried. She was the first to reach him after the ambush when he lost his mares. She says the papers he carried proved his name was Rock Wesley and that he owned the Morgan mares."

Henry Sale decided that he was in over his depth. He turned abruptly toward the door, mumbling, "I'll talk to you later—right now I've got things to do."

One of the men in the room got to the door before he did and stood there, blocking his way. And Blake said, "Not yet, sheriff. We haven't finished talking to you."

In Roy Seigel's office, all the movable furniture had been piled against the walls and on either side of the door. The entrance, itself, was open.

"That's to let them in if any of them want to come in," Wallace said to Meg, his eyes crinkling. "But I've a notion most of 'em will be satisfied to stay out in the street and pump lead this way."

For a while there had been the threat of flames from the burning barn, but the townsmen had organized a bucket brigade as soon as the shooting had died, to put out the blaze before it spread to engulf the rest of the town.

Indian Charlie was standing near the door in an attitude of listening.

"Hear anything, Charlie?" Rock asked.

The Indian shook his head.

Rock turned and came over to Meg. He led her to a chair and said, "You might as well sit down. We've got to wait."

"You don't seem at all excited," Meg said. "None of you seem excited. You act as though you did this every day."

Rock laughed. "Not me—and I think I can answer for Jeff. But Ken's had some rough times. So has Charlie."

"How did Charlie get Ken out of jail?"

"He didn't. Ken can pick any lock that ever was made. What Charlie did was take care of the guard who had been left at the jail, and furnish guns for Ken and Roy and the two drifters after they got out."

Ken Wallace joined them, and Rock said, "Ken, what am I going to do with this girl? She's got to know everything, have a part in everything, and worse than that, she has opinions."

"Marry her," Ken said chuckling.

"I intend to," Rock said. "But how'll I handle her?"

"You won't, but you'll have some beautiful fights trying to."

Jinny came in from the back room with Doc Brubaker. "He'll he riding his horse in three days," Doc Brubaker said.

"I've got a gash in the back you can look at," Rock said.

"You didn't tell me!" Meg cried.

"It doesn't amount to much."

He peeled off his coat and shirt and straddled a chair while Brubaker applied salve and bandage.

"You're Wesley, aren't you?" Brubaker said after he finished. "Or should I call you Ringo Lafferty?"

"The name's Wesley," Rock said.

"Chenoweth doesn't think so," Brubaker said. "He's going to be heading this way any minute now. Looks like I'll have more work to do before the day's over."

"Unless you stop him," Rock said.

"Stop Chenoweth. No one's ever stopped him. He thinks he owns everything around here."

There was a bitter note in the doctor's voice. He picked up his bag, shrugged, and turned toward the door.

"Stop in at father's store on the way to your office," Jinny called. "Tell him I'm here again, and that I'm staying here. On the way to get you, I told him why."

"I'll tell him, Jinny," Brubaker said.

Jinny smiled. She looked at Rock and said, "Father doesn't approve of what I'm doing, but like a good many other people, he's fed up with Chenoweth, too."

She turned, then, and hurried to the back room.

Indian Charlie backed away from the street door. He said, "Men coming, Rock."

Rock Wesley nodded. He glanced at Meg and smiled, but his smile was forced. They were set up to hold out as long as possible, but he wasn't at all sure how long that would be. The barricades along the walls would keep back some of the bullets, but some would come through.

Meg wasn't deceived. "Our chances aren't very good, are they, Rock?"

"We're not whipped yet. Get over there back of the desk, Meg. I'll join you in a minute, after I make a check of the back room."

Chenoweth's crowd moved boldly up the street. Near their destination, some took shelter at building corners across the way and some circled to the rear. But Chenoweth, Jake Leydon, Bealer Harrison, and a few more, stopped in front of the adjoining building. And from there, Chenoweth made his demands.

"Lafferty, come on out. Give up now, and we guarantee you a fair trial," he shouted. "Make a fight of it and you won't live that long."

No one from Seigel's office made any answer.

"Did you hear me, Lafferty?" Chenoweth roared. "Do we have to come in and get you?"

There still was no answer from Seigel's.

Chenoweth waited half a minute, then lifted his arm in a signal to the men across the street. A rifle bullet ripped into the front wall of the attorney's office, another crashed through one of the front windows. Two screamed through the open door. Firing started in the rear, lacing into the back room.

Rock Wesley, peering over the desk, snapped a shot at a man across the street. Kneeling near him, Indian Charlie started firing steadily, and from the other side of the room, Ken Wallace, Jeff Elliott, and Roy Seigel poured back shot for shot.

Meg handed Indian Charlie a freshly loaded gun. She took the one he had emptied and started reloading it. They had the guns and ammunition they had taken from the prisoners in the barn—all the guns and ammunition they would need.

The firing grew heavier. It continued for almost a full minute, then stopped. Rock heard a crash as the back door broke in. He came to his feet, rushed back and saw three men in the entrance, one of them Jake Leydon. Two had swung their guns on Jim Fleming, lying behind a filing cabinet at the far end of the room.

Rock fired from the hip. Someone sided him—Ken Wallace. One of those in the doorway pitched forward on his face. Leydon half turned and sank to the floor. The third man reeled back out of sight.

Wallace muttered something under his breath, dropped to his knees, then stretched out full length.

"Front door!" Jeff screamed.

Rock whirled. His gunhammer clicked on an empty shell. Shots whipped past him as he dived to where Meg was lying, and reached toward her for a loaded gun. Indian Charlie, half crouching, and Jeff Elliott had those in the doorway in a cross fire. As suddenly as the men had appeared there, they were gone.

Rock wiped his arm across his face. He crawled to where Ken Wallace was lying and drew him to a place of safety. There were two bullets in Wallace, one in his shoulder and one through the side. He was unconscious, but the wounds were not necessarily fatal.

Rock pulled off his coat, took off his shirt, and started ripping it to make temporary bandages. "Charlie," he called. "See what happened in the back room."

Indian Charlie scurried away.

The firing had started again from outside. It was a steady, raking fire, this time, and at a guess, it might be continued for a long time. Chenoweth's first attempt to smash them had failed, and had been costly. Before he tried it again he would want to cut some of them down.

Indian Charlie came crawling back. "They all right," he said, referring to Jinny and Fleming in the back room.

Meg helped Rock tie packs over Ken Wallace's wounds. Her hands were steady but there wasn't much color in her face.

"They'll try again?" she whispered.

"Maybe," Rock said bleakly.

He checked the gun Meg had given him, wondering how long they would be able to hold out. That he hadn't taken a bullet in the exchange with Jake Leyden was a miracle. He couldn't count on being as lucky next time.

The firing eased up, stopped.

A voice from the street shouted, "Wesley—Wesley. I'm coming in."

He looked at Meg and managed a grin. He said, "I'm Wesley, now. They've forgotten I'm supposed to be an outlaw named Lafferty."

"That sounded like Henry Sale," Meg said.

Rock wondered where Henry Sale had found the nerve to take part in the fight, but he shouted back, "Come ahead, Sale."

The sheriff wasn't alone when he appeared in the doorway. Several men were with him. Rock looked at them sharply, not recognizing any as men who rode for Chenoweth. One was the bartender he had talked to in the Long Shot saloon, one was Carl Blake, Jinny's father. One was the young fellow from the feed store, Fred

Brady. One was a rancher he had met, named Sam Dobell. He lowered the gun he was holding, and asked, bluntly, "What is it you want?"

It was Bradley, the bartender who stepped forward. "No sense in this fight going on any longer," Bradley said. "We just had a talk with Chenoweth, an' told him so. He claims you're an outlaw named Lafferty. You claim he stole some mares of yours and that you know where he's holding them. That right?"

"That's right," Rock said. He tried to keep his voice steady. He could guess what had happened. The people here in Modoc had stepped in between him and Chenoweth, for this was their town, and its welfare was their business.

"It should be easy to determine who's lying," Bradley said. "A couple of us are ready to ride with you to see if those mares really exist. The rest of us, to the number of about thirty, are pledged to keep the peace until we get the answer. We're calling on you to surrender. Your men can have the run of the Long Shot saloon. Chenoweth's crowd is to stay in the Golden Horseshoe. Your wounded will be cared for. Then, when we get back from our trip, someone goes to jail. Do you agree to those terms?"

Here was a promise of complete vindication and victory. He couldn't have asked for more. Meg was standing near him. He reached for her hand, and nodded.

"Sure, Bradley."

Blake hurried forward, looking frightened. "Where's my daughter?"

Rock told him, and watched him hurry to the back room, then glanced at Meg.

"Nothing to worry about any more," she whispered.

He shook his head. "No, nothing to worry about any more."

18

Chenoweth couldn't understand what had happened, or how it happened. When a crowd of men had come marching up the street, apparently led by the sheriff, his first thought had been that here were the men he needed to wipe out the resistance of those who were pinned down in Seigel's. It had surprised him that Frank Bradley spoke up instead of the sheriff, and to Bradley's demands he had made an angry, blustering denial.

But Bradley wasn't alone in wanting what he wanted. Blake and Dobell and Brady, and half a dozen more had crowded around him showing no respect at all. Their guns had covered him. And facing a situation such as that, what could he do but seem to give in?

Damn it, he would remember every man in the crowd—and later he would exact payment for what they had done. This, he promised himself, but even as he made the promise an uneasy doubt had started nagging him.

Bradley had told him that a few men from town were going to make a quick ride to the Arrowhead to see if he was holding Wesley's lost mares. Let them. In a ride to the ranch they wouldn't find the mares. In a week of searching they wouldn't find them. Yet, when he had said that, Bradley had seemed awfully confident. Why? Was it possible that someone here in town knew where he was hiding them? Or had one of his men sold out?

He shifted uneasily in his chair. He glanced around the room. Eleven of his men were here in the Golden Horseshoe with him. Three had been killed. Five were wounded seriously and several had superficial scratches. Damn it, that crowd from Sawtelle had put up quite a fight. They had made it so tough that some of the men, who usually loved a good battle, were acting fed up with it.

He finished his drink, poured another, but pushed it away, untouched. This was no time to be drinking. Right now, if ever in his life, he needed a clear head. "Bealer!" he shouted. "Bealer, come here!"

Bealer Harrison left the bar, came to his table and sat down.

"How the hell did Wallace and Seigel get out of jail?" he asked bluntly.

"Marshall, who was there on guard, told me an Indian jumped him."

"An Indian!" Chenoweth snorted. "There's no Indian in Modoc—in the entire valley."

"This one came from Sawtelle, with Wallace. He hasn't been around town much, but Jake Leydon saw him on the hotel porch when he arrested Wallace. Jake was wondering if he shouldn't have arrested the Indian, too. I think he knows where we've got the mares."

Chenoweth caught his breath. "You think they know where we're hiding the Morgans?"

"They either know for sure, or they've got a good idea. I'm betting they know. And I'm not in favor of sticking in here much longer. I've no liking for jails."

"We're not going to jail," Chenoweth said sharply. "None of us."

"It's almost dark," Harrison said. "The men who rode to the Arrowhead got away by two o'clock. If they knew where to ride, they could be back here before very long."

Chenoweth forgot his decision to stop drinking. He reached for his glass, downed it, then sank lower in his chair, scowling, and slipping into the dark, ugly mood which had held him most of the afternoon. Damn it, he wasn't finished. Even if the stolen mares had been found, he wasn't through. He had a crowd of fighting men to back him up. The courage of men like Bradley, Blake, Dobell and those who had joined them this afternoon, didn't run very deep. In the past, they had jumped at his commands. They would again.

What he had to do now was strike at the heart of their temporary rebellion, and there was one quick way to do it. Wesley and the men from Sawtelle had carried most of the fight up to now. Wallace, he had heard, had been wounded. If he could take care of Wesley, where would that leave the rebels? They'd have an old Indian and a cowhand named Elliott to lead them.

He rubbed his hands together. He was beginning to feel better. His mind seemed unusually clear. Kill Wesley, and plaster him again with the name of Ringo Lafferty. See that the cowhand and the Indian were taken care of, individually. Who would be left to claim the mares? No one. He could forge the papers to prove they were his—and then he could go after men like Bradley. He could do it cleverly, but effectively. Bradley, for instance, he could hit through Edna. He could get the bank to call Sam Dobell's loans. Hell, he had all the tools he needed to come out on top again.

But first, he had to handle Wesley, and that was going to be pure pleasure. Wesley and Meg McAlpin. He owed her something too. He would have her on her knees before he finished with her.

He took another drink, then stood up, and laughed. He wasn't at all unsteady. The drinking he had done hadn't hurt him. He checked his gun, slid it back in its holster, and stared at Bealer Harrison.

"Stay here," he ordered. "Keep the men here. When I get back we'll move out and show this town a thing or two."

"There are men guarding the front door, and the back," Harrison said.

"To hell with them," Chenoweth said. "I'll leave by one of the windows."

It was dark by the time the men returned from the Arrowhead. They went at once to the Long Chance saloon. Indian Charlie, who had been with them, nodded to Rock as they came in.

Bradley's eyes were glowing. "They were there, Wesley," he declared. "And although I don't know much about horses, I could see they were something special."

"I know Morgans," Sam Dobell said. "They looked worth fighting for."

"It wasn't the Morgans I was fighting for," Rock said. "It was the two men who died in the ambush."

Bradley turned toward the door, then looked back. "We'll get our crowd together and go over to the Golden Horseshoe. We'll have a talk with Chenoweth, but no matter what he says, he'll be on his way to jail ten minutes after we get there. I never thought I'd live to see the day when Chenoweth went to jail, but that day has come. A great day for Modoc."

"Do we have to stay here?" Rock asked. "I'd like to check at the doctor's and see how Wallace and Fleming are making out. Then I ought to take Meg to her sister's."

"You'll drop in here later?"

"Sure."

"Then go ahead, but steer clear of the Golden Horseshoe. Chenoweth is our problem now. What we're doing tonight we should have done long ago."

Indian Charlie and Jeff Elliott went along to Dr. Brubaker's, where the report on Wallace and Fleming was as good as they could have expected. Wallace was asleep, but resting easily, and in no danger. "He might even be able to travel in a week or ten days," Doc Brubaker told them. "Fleming's got even better medicine. They make quite a pair, he and Jinny."

From the doctor's, Indian Charlie and Jeff headed back to the Long Chance, while Rock and Meg started toward her sister's home. They walked slowly.

"I'm glad of the way it worked out for Jinny and Jim," Meg said. "Her father came between them once—I think he half convinced her that Jim didn't have much get-up and go. He couldn't have been more wrong."

"Until I saw how they felt about each other, I thought Fleming was in love with you," Rock said.

"He was mildly interested, but that's all. If I had married him I would have been substituting for Jinny. I wouldn't like to be a substitute."

"You never will be with me," Rock said.

"Are you really taking me to Sawtelle?"

"Really."

"Then don't you think you ought to make love to me, or something?"

"Like this?"

He stopped, and took her in his arms. It was dark and silent on the side street and he held her for a long time. It was Meg who finally pushed him away, and who said, laughing softly.

"I think I'll like it in Sawtelle."

They walked on, but stopped again in front of her sister's.

"I wish father could have known how things would work out," Meg said. "But I think he guessed."

"I'm sure he did."

He put both hands on her shoulders and stood looking down into her face. It was dark, but the stars gave enough light so that he could see her smile. He drew her closer, and said, "Meg—"

Something stopped him—some sound which scarcely registered in his mind, but which he had heard—unless it was some instinctive sense of danger. He stopped and stood listening, his eyes probing the darkness beyond her and to either side.

"What is it, Rock?"

He shook his head. "I don't know. Nothing, maybe. When can I see you in the morning?"

"As early as you want to call."

"For breakfast, then. Right after sun-up. Can I invite myself to be your guest?"

"Let me invite you."

He laughed softly, and nodded. "I'll be on your porch when the sun comes up."

He kissed her, but held her in his arms for only a moment. He stood watching as she walked toward the house. He heard her knock on the door, saw it open, and saw her figure outlined against the light of the room as she turned and waved. A moment later the door closed behind her.

What was bothering him? What was it that had made his muscles tense, his senses scream a warning? A faint, scraping sound caught his attention. It seemed to come from somewhere behind him, and was the kind of sound that might have been made by the shifting of a man's foot. He brushed back his coat, his hand dropping to rest on the butt of his holstered gun.

He got his answer almost immediately.

A low, grating voice spoke his name and issued a command.

"Wesley! Turn around, Wesley!"

He didn't move. He guessed, instantly, who stood there in the darkness behind him. It was Arne Chenoweth. In some way or other the man had slipped out of the Golden Horseshoe, and had come here to wait for him, sure he would walk home with Meg.

Chenoweth spoke again. "Wesley, turn around. I've got something for you—a bullet to smash your face in. Turn around."

Rock hardly heard what the man said. He was concentrating his attention on exactly where the voice came from, on where Chenoweth would be standing. It was his only hope.

He took a deep breath. He knew he couldn't delay his turn much longer. In fact he was a little surprised that Chenoweth had spoken at all, but perhaps the man's egotism was so demanding he had to feed it. In this way, he could boast in the days ahead of having given his enemy a chance.

Once more Chenoweth spoke, his words seeming to come from behind Rock and slightly to the left. And this time there was an edge of annoyance in his voice. "Turn, damn it! Or you can have it in the back!"

Rock didn't wait an instant longer. He swung sideways, dropping into a crouch and whipping his gun free of its holster. There was a burst of orange flame. He felt a stinging blow against the side of his face as he squeezed the trigger, driving a bullet at the hulking figure of Arne Chenoweth. He saw the blossom of flame again as he fired a second time. Something struck him high in the chest and a numbing pain started spreading through his body.

He was on the ground, now, although he didn't remember falling. He fired a third time, then fired once more, and finally lay motionless. He thought he could see another motionless figure on the ground, where Arne Chenoweth had been crouching, but he wasn't sure.

The house door had burst open and Meg had come out on the porch. She cried out his name and came running down the path toward him.

"Go back, Meg," he whispered.

But she didn't go back, and a moment later was kneeling beside him.

Alice and her husband came out, and Brady hurried to where Chenoweth had fallen. He stooped over him, then after a moment straightened up, shaking his head.

"This ends it," he said flatly. "Tomorrow will be a new day. How's Rock?"

"Help me get him inside," Meg said. "Then go for the doctor."

"Don't fuss over me," Rock growled.

"I'll fuss over you if I want to," Meg answered. "Be quiet."

Rock shook his head. "I'll never get over it. What's a woman always want to fight for—" He closed his eyes. His head rested on something very soft.

The last things he saw were Meg's tearful eyes, and the gentle smile tugging at her lips. He wanted to see them again, but was damned if he would open his eyes again until she asked him.

He had a pretty good idea she would ask him.

Center Point Large Print
600 Brooks Road / PO Box 1
Thorndike, ME 04986-0001 USA

(207) 568-3717

US & Canada:
1 800 929-9108
www.centerpointlargeprint.com